BLOOD FAERIE

INDIA DRUMMOND

Blood Faerie

Second edition published in the United Kingdom 2013 by India Drummond

ISBN-13: 978-1492226420
ISBN-10: 1492226424

Author contact:
http://www.indiadrummond.com/

Acknowledgements

There is one person that without his help, this book truly would not have happened: Inspector Dorian Marshall of the Tayside Police. I always wanted to write a main character as a police officer, but feared that, by error or omission, I would insult every cop of every rank in every locale in Scotland by getting it wrong. Inspector Marshall kept that from happening. His patient and thorough advice made this book stronger. Any errors in fact or procedure are completely my own, although I did my best to do him proud.

In addition, I'm certain there's a special place in heaven for my family, friends, and beta readers, who give me the support and confidence to keep writing one story after another.

Fae Name Pronunciation Guide

In order of appearance:

Eilidh: AY-lee

Cridhe: CREED

Imire: em-IRE

Saor: SAY-or

Dudlach: DOOD-lawk

Krostach: CROST-ack

Beniss: BEN-iss

Oron: oh-RON

Galen: GAY-len

Genoa: JEN-oh-uh

CHAPTER 1

EILIDH DETECTED THE GREASY SCENT of evil moments before she heard the scream below. She perched in St Paul's steeple, watching Perth's late night pub-crawlers through rotting slats. The scurrying footfalls of humans did not hold her interest, nor did the seeping ruby blood that spread quickly over the flat, grey paving stones. Instead, her eyes turned north along Methven Street, seeking the source of that familiar smell.

Evil smelled like nothing else, worse than a rotting corpse, worse than sewage and disease, more vile than the fumes that billowed from modern machinery, more cloying than the shame of drunken whores. This particular evil was fresh, but not quite pure. It mixed with rage but was contained, refined, as though gestated in the belly of ancient hatred. This evil held promise, and for the first time in decades, Eilidh hesitated, slightly afraid.

The familiar magic that nestled in the subtle overtones of this particular wrong propelled her into action. She pulled back the shutter and leapt down to the roof below. Her feet made scarcely a sound as she landed on the mossy stone. She ensured that the black sweatshirt hood covered her short white hair and the other tell-tale signs of her race. Moving faster than any human could, she skipped down the side of the building, lightly touching window frames and door tops until she landed on the hidden south side of the dilapidated octagonal church.

The corpse at her feet stared at the full moon, glassy-eyed and empty. She crouched beside it and sniffed the air. The hole hacked in his chest left bone and organ exposed. Blood poured from it. He'd passed by the church only moments before. Eilidh had seen him with a human female who leaned against him, taking drunken steps, screeching too loudly, laughing at nothing. Eilidh had paid neither of them any attention. They were like scores of others who staggered down her street most nights.

Her senses caught the earliest whiff of decay. It began immediately upon death, as soon as the heart no longer thrust blood through mortal veins. Eilidh had to move before it masked the trace she hunted. She sprang forward and her feet carried her north just as someone behind her shouted, "Oi! You!"

The scent was not difficult to track. She darted past the small groupings of oblivious people, mostly gathering in the doorways of pubs, smoke wafting from their mouths. Various human smells: sweat, smoke, cars, and food all mingled together, but none could distract Eilidh from her quarry. She knew this smell because it was old and magical, and, like her, it was fae.

She followed the trace past the main thoroughfare, taking only minimal care not to attract attention. Habit made her duck and dodge away from people. Although she was faster, better trained, and had keener senses, human technology could render those advantages moot.

Her handmade leather shoes made no sound as she pursued the unknown faerie down dark, cobbled side streets. Once, she'd stolen human shoes, but the same day she left them near the entrance of a homeless shelter. She could not bear the feel of the strange rubber. It squeaked and smelled of oil. So she'd made shoes in the style of her own people, using the hide of a lamb she'd killed near Kinnoull Hill, a woodland area she rarely dared visit. Its cliff summit overlooked the city, but the proximity to the fae kingdom made it dangerous. The shoes, moulded over time by her weak earth magic, would be thought quaint or foreign. They were the only item she wore that was not distinctly human, but they never slipped on tile rooftops, so she took the risk of them being noticed.

Eilidh could not help but wonder about the faerie she chased. Did he too try to blend into human society? Was he exiled as she was, or born of an outcast? Had she known him in her other life? Before she was cursed to live where the ground was hard with pavement and the air polluted with fumes, the scent of foul human food, and the sound of endless, meaningless chatter?

She crossed a street, easily dodging cars that roared past. Then Eilidh stepped into the shadows, her back hugging a tall tree on the North Inch, a square mile of manicured green on the edge of the city, now cast in complete darkness. Her heart beat rapidly within her chest.

Tugging back her hood, she listened hard. A dog barked. A distant siren howled. A human ran along the circular track around the park. The water of the River Tay lapped gently against its banks. Cars crossed the Old Bridge.

Eilidh whispered to the night. *A'shalei tedrecht.* Nothing. It was risky, casting with another of her race nearby, perhaps even watching, and her ability was weak. But the scent had dissipated. It had led her this way and then disappeared. She doubted the traffic alone could have so completely obscured the scent.

Walking across the green to the water's edge, Eilidh could not resist the pull that drew her eyes to the hills. Beyond them lay the kingdom that had cast her out. The order had been "kill on sight." It would never be lifted. The fae did not forgive or forget. Her crime was in her blood, and there could be no restitution.

She pulled the hood to cover the long, twisted points of her ears and headed back to St Paul's. The crumbling church had been her home for nearly a quarter of a century. Townspeople wanted it torn down. Developers wanted it turned into a wine bar or an art museum. Eilidh wanted a place where she could watch. She would have her way, and the humans would never understand why all their plans fell through. She might feel sorry for them if she cared, but she did not.

Blue lights flashed into her sensitive silver-green eyes. She cut through Mill Wynd, slithering along two-hundred-year-old stone walls to watch the commotion below. Men in bright yellow jackets stood in groups of two and three, behind a cordon they'd placed around the body. Eilidh listened to their chatter with curiosity. She caught words like "butcher", which confused her. No meat-seller had done this. Could they not recognise evil when they saw it so plainly manifested?

She was dismayed that they could not smell what she had tracked, but at the same time, relief filled her. Whatever had done this was not of their world, and they would not have the means to deal with it. For them to try to hunt this thing would only mean many human deaths. In theory, Eilidh did not mind human deaths any more than she regretted the death of the lamb whose skin she wore on her feet, but she did not like the idea of a predator in her city, feeding on innocence, killing to nourish darkness.

It had been twenty-five years since Eilidh had borne the weight of any responsibility except to feed herself. She was no longer a Watcher. She could ignore it. Easily. The evil might move on. The dark faerie might not return. But even as the thought formed, she knew it was not true. Some twisted creature of her own kind had come into the city to hunt or to steal. The humans could not stop it. Only she could.

She cast her eyes to the north, to the half-mile back where she'd lost the scent. When her gaze returned to the human police, she saw one looking directly at her. She swore. *Faith.* Slamming her back into the stone, she felt him approach, heard the thunk of his rubber-soled shoes against the concrete as he inched closer. He was wary; she could smell sweat and uncertainty. From the darkness, she turned to face him and raised her chin enough to peer out from under the black hood. A flash of something passed over his face. Something in his expression paralysed her for an instant. Instead of being repelled by her magic, he seemed drawn to it. Worse yet, he saw her eyes.

He hesitated only a moment before he said, "Don't be afraid, son. I just want to ask you a couple of questions."

Because she was taller than the average human female and slight of frame, city people often mistook her for a teenaged boy. That she wore a hooded sweatshirt and dark jeans helped the illusion. She slipped away, skirting around the building to a small car park behind her. Rolling to the ground, she darted underneath a squat red vehicle. She hated the stench of machinery. Even after so long in the city, she couldn't accept the smells that invaded her keen nose on a daily basis. She breathed the word, *deny*.

His shoes passed quickly, but he paused as though sensing her. Was that possible? She had been a Watcher, and she knew how to track and go unseen. No human could detect her magic, and yet, this one hesitated. His worn black shoes stopped directly in front of her. If she'd wanted to, she could have reached out and traced a finger along his laces, or lashed out and broken his ankles, depending on her mood.

She had no desire to hurt the human and knew if she did, it would only bring more police. She dismissed the idea that he might capture her. Humans were bigger, yes, and stronger, of course, but Eilidh was not defenceless. She hid only to protect her secrets.

Most fae could pass for human on cursory inspection, and depending on their colouring, some even at close range. But no human could stare deep into her eyes and not sense the Otherworld. The locals had an expression, "a fey look." It wasn't too far off the mark. Her white hair could be a wig or dye. But her eyes had flecks of silver that swam with the magic of her people. Her blood was pure and her lineage ancient.

The police officer's feet turned after a few long moments. He walked up and down the car park, nearly all the way to the old mill. Eilidh didn't move. She knew how to be patient. She'd stalked both deer and men for hours. Eventually he gave up and returned to St Paul's Square. When he did, she followed in the shadows.

∞

Cridhe trembled, his eyes fixed to the south, his blood coursing with power. The tension in his limbs relaxed as he released the darkness that hid him. When that beautiful warrior had spoken her enchantment, she'd teased the edges of his power. It had aroused him even further. Considering that his skin already tingled and every sense, both physical and magical, was heightened from the kill, it shocked him that any sight could distract him. He anticipated the delights to come later that night and recalled the unbearable pleasure of every past sacrifice. Still her memory tugged his attention. *But why?* He'd heard of the outcast, naturally. He had not expected to encounter her or to be both pursued by and drawn to her.

A siren started some miles in the distance and drew closer. *How could she stand living among them?* Under the best of circumstances, he loathed the noises humans made with their cars and trains, but tonight the wail screamed in his thrumming ears. He had to get away from the city to finish what he'd started. Cridhe had little difficulty evading the kingdom Watchers. His blood magic closed their ears and eyes to his presence.

He inhaled deeply and let the scent of fresh blood fill his nose. His fingers went to the pouch that hung across his body, and caressed the human heart that still beat through the power of his blood magic. His essence throbbed with vitality so fierce he caught his breath. Suddenly consumed with hunger, Cridhe turned and left the city behind.

CHAPTER 2

POLICE CONSTABLE QUINTON MUNRO
stopped dead in his tracks. He could have sworn he
heard tapping behind him, but when he turned, he
saw no one.

"Spooked, eh?"

Munro sought out the speaker, expecting a ribbing
from his partner, but even though Getty's voice was
full of bravado, his face was pale and shaken. They'd
been first on the scene. "It's a dead vicious one, that,"
Munro said.

"Aye," Getty agreed.

Munro fought the urge to turn again. He might have
convinced himself he'd imagined the sounds, if it
weren't for a prickling on the back of his skull. He
felt as though he was being watched. Things like
that happened, and he knew not to dismiss it, no
matter how tempting it might be. His sergeant said
he was both the unluckiest bastard on the force and

the luckiest. The other coppers called him *haunted*. He'd like to chalk it up to luck, but luck was only supposed to sneak up on you every once in a while, to explain the inexplicable. It didn't hang around your neck like a bloody millstone.

So nobody was surprised when Munro called in that he was on scene within moments of an emergency treble-nine call. When he'd told Getty to take a left off Atholl while returning to the station after a domestic, Getty didn't argue. In fact, his partner didn't seem to think twice. Munro had a difficult time not telling him to hurry.

Sometimes a bad feeling nagged. Other times a hunch would twist his gut. This one screamed in his head and clawed the insides of his eyes.

Sergeant Hallward barked his name as he approached the *Police Do Not Cross* tape protecting the crime scene. The sergeant pulled Munro and Getty aside and nodded, waiting for their report.

"Sarge. At 20:45 we were passing and I noticed a man." Munro consulted a small, blue notebook. "Gregory Johnson, yelling and waving his hands to flag us down."

Hallward interrupted. "You were passing." Not a question. More a statement saying he knew they were in an unusual place at an unusual time.

"Aye. I'd wanted to stop at the chippie," Munro said. They both knew he was lying, but it was for the best. When the sergeant nodded, Munro continued. "Mr Johnson showed us the body. Said he'd just called 999. Getty secured the scene while I called it in." Munro hadn't wanted to call it in, but if he'd balked, he'd have to face that it was because of his damned "luck."

He was fast gaining a reputation for always being on the spot of the worst crimes. Just once, he wanted to ignore the pull, but instincts like this one were always right. Not usually...*always*. Every time he felt it, he wanted to keep going and let some other sod be first on the scene. Then he'd reminded himself why he became a copper to begin with. One day, he thought, he'd get there before disaster struck, and he'd prevent someone from having the worst night of his life.

His gaze went to the body. It lay as they'd found it. Soon SOCO, the scenes of crime officers, would arrive and put a white tent over the gruesome display. "We have a name?" he asked Sergeant Hallward. Munro hadn't touched the body to search for ID, but forensics and CID, the Criminal Investigation Department, were en route and would be there within minutes. Impressive, considering how few murders Perth saw. Domestic abuse and drug related crime, they saw those every day, but this was different. The shock on the victim's face wasn't something Munro would forget any time soon. Nor was the savage rip in the chest or the smell that poured from it.

"CID will check it out," Hallward said. His eyes searched Munro's.

"Vicious." Munro repeated the assessment he'd made earlier to Getty. "Seems personal."

Getty spoke up. "Can't get much more personal than ripping someone's heart out."

Munro turned to the sergeant. "A lad was hanging about a few minutes ago. Took off like a light when I approached. Fourteen, fifteen maybe. Skinny kid. Maybe he saw something. Could have just been a nosy bugger, but I got a feeling." Munro shrugged. He didn't like talking about his hunches. "Be a bastard to find though. Dark jeans and a hood. Didn't get a good look at his face. Had light eyes." Those eyes had latched on to Munro and made his gut lurch.

Hallward nodded at Getty. "Did you see him?"

"Not his face. Scarpered pretty quick." Getty gestured toward Mill Street.

"He wasn't one of the usuals. Clothes were baggy, but clean," Munro said.

An ambulance pulled up, immediately followed by two other cars. Munro recognised Detective Inspector Boyle and Detective Sergeant Hayes as the two CID officers, as well as the Home Office pathologist.

A drop fell from the sky and landed on Munro's shoulder, quickly followed by another.

"Bloody hell," someone said.

Sergeant Hallward turned to Munro and Getty. "Going to be a long night."

Forensic technicians dressed in protective white jumpsuits worked quickly to take pictures and collect evidence before the coming rain washed away something the murderer left behind. The three policemen stayed on the cordon to protect the scene as the SOCOs did their job.

A strange flurry above him made Munro glance up.

"Fuckin' pigeons," Getty said and shrugged with a hard scowl etched on his face.

For just a moment, Munro wondered if Getty could also sense they were being watched. He let his eyes wander to the walls of the other buildings around the little square. The glare of the scene lights made it hard to see anything but gloom.

∞

A light pressure tapped Eilidh's toe. She looked down in the darkness of the church steeple, and a smile flitted across her tense mouth. "It's you, is it? Where have you been? I thought the barber next door must've finally caught you. He's been after you for weeks, you know." She'd not had much difficulty getting past the policemen. Humans saw what they wanted to see, and she'd been careful to approach the church from the opposite side.

Crouching low, she pulled a few crumbs from her pocket and offered them to the rat. He came close, unafraid, and Eilidh scratched behind his ear. With twitching whiskers, he chattered with appreciation. His feet tapped the wooden planks as he retreated to the building's lower levels.

Eilidh stood again and peered outside, fascinated that her quiet street had become such a hive of activity. Blue lights flashed, and they'd cordoned off Old High Street Wynd, blocking what little traffic went by. The vehicle movement had slowed in recent years, since the humans put up signs telling each other to drive only in one direction. It amazed her that they could be so organised and follow arbitrary rules of which way to face, but despite her doubts, they saw the blue arrows and red circles and obeyed. The fae never used signs or markers. Magical boundaries told them all they needed to know.

She watched three policemen below. One was taller than the other two. He was broad and erect like a stone wall. In her time in the human city, she'd noticed the police often had that stance, as if making themselves oak-like would deter wrongdoers. Perhaps it did.

The people were so different, and even after a quarter of a century in this tiny tower, watching them every day, Eilidh did not truly understand them. Fae warriors were silent, agile, and their greatest strength came from their ability to channel the seasons. Stature was irrelevant to power. She'd watched the humans through their windows, but never entered a human home. She saw them on the streets, but never engaged them in conversation. Her fate was to be apart.

To hear her father Imire tell it, at one time the fae got along well with humans, back before Scotland was called Caledonia and before the Picts came under the rule of one God. Those people had understood the power of the Elder Race. Eilidh's brow furrowed as she remembered her father's voice and the way he would mutter about modern humans. Her gaze went to the dense clouds that dropped rain on the scene below. Her father loved rain. His strength came from the second season, and he knew how to draw from water. Rain held the element of air and the earth rose to meet it, bringing the power of the first and third seasons with it.

When Eilidh looked down again, the humans were walking away. She caught the sounds of their speech, and she recognised the one who'd spoken to her, the one who'd seen through her shadows. A name drifted to her from the lips of the soldier-like policeman. He called the other Munro. The word tickled at her ear and found its way to her lips. "Munro," she whispered.

She had not intended to put power into the word, but the instant it left her mouth, he turned and cast his eyes upward. She stepped into the shadows, her heart pounding. She'd heard of true druids, in stories her father told, but thought they must have died out, as humans turned away from magic and embraced invention. When Eilidh inched forward again, he no longer looked toward her. They had greeted another group of policemen, and they all swarmed around the human carcass. She suddenly felt vulnerable in her spire. She climbed down to a more central level of the church, angry at the murderous faerie that brought this disruption to her doorstep.

Anger was a sensation Eilidh had rarely experienced before her exile. Her father tried to protect her when everyone learned the secret of her forbidden magical talents, but what more could he have done? What choice did they have? The fae didn't have prisons. When the death order came, her father had visited on the pretence of allowing her to consecrate her soul to the Earth. No one suspected her father, the upright priest, would send her on the run. All would consider that fate worse than finding the peaceful embrace of the Mother.

"I didn't teach you enough about humans," was all he said when he entered the room where she'd been left under guard.

"You taught me nothing about them."

"Come, Eilidh. It is time to pay tribute to the Mother."

So, it would be tonight. She remembered staring straight into the guard's eyes as they passed. He had tensed, and she felt a small pleasure in knowing he was afraid of her, even though her father held her inside a binding bubble that cut her off from the Ways of Earth. The pleasure was short lived when she considered that he thought her to be a monster.

I did not mean to cast the azure.

Soon, she and her father stood within the stone circle. He released the binding and put up a shield of magic around the stones. "The binding would be an affront to the Mother," he said. "None can be brought into Her presence against their will." It had been Imire's way to explain his every action to her. Even at her Rite of Final Prayers, he still instructed her.

A thick elm branch rested beside one of the stones. "Father," she said. "The circle is broken by that branch." She felt removed and distant, considering the ritual academically and not as her last opportunity to reconcile with the Goddess. But in her disbelief of all that had happened, she could not touch the emotions trapped within. *Could this really be happening?*

"Yes," Imire said with a heavy sigh. "You must strike me with it to break my shielding, but not yet."

Eilidh's mind froze, not willing to grasp what she must do. How could she attack her own father in a holy place? Where would she go?

He turned to her with a tender expression. "I have been a distant father. I should have instructed you better. And now there is no time to make up for my failings." He glanced up at the cloudy sky, his eyes shining like river crystals. "Remain within the human cities where our people's power has faded to nothing."

"You want me to run."

"I was a fool." His face was smooth and beautiful, but she saw the age in his eyes as he spoke. "Eilidh..." He tucked a tiny package into her hand. "I'm sorry I cannot give you more."

Eilidh was paralyzed. "Father, I can't go." She was not eager to die, but living outside the kingdom? She'd seen the barbarian humans from a distance. What she saw sickened her.

The expression in his blue eyes turned sharp. "Survive." His gaze flicked to the branch, and he turned to face the northern stone. For his sake, the conclave had to believe she'd overpowered him. She hit him hard enough to break his shield and incapacitate him, and she prayed to the Mother that he would survive.

To this day, she did not know if he lived. Up until that moment, she'd been innocent. When she ran, she confirmed her guilt. Her father had cursed her to live between worlds, never a part of either.

She had been a child, not yet past her first century. She'd celebrated that milestone of adulthood alone with the pigeons and rats in the abandoned St Paul's. The evil that had brushed her doorstep made her wish for the first time in decades for her father's counsel. He would have known what to do.

The order against her still stood: kill on sight. She'd never get close to her father. He rarely came anywhere near the borders and spent much of his time in the Otherworld. But perhaps there was another of her kind who would stay the order long enough for her to get word to Imire. She needed to take the chance, to ask his advice, and to warn the conclave of this renegade faerie. *Perhaps.*

The killer would not stop with taking one human life. The forbidden magic of the Path of the Azure was addictive, as she well knew, and this murder had obviously been aided by a blood spell. Azuri magic had two possible manifestations, blood or astral magic. The Ways of Earth and its air, water, stone, and fire magic could not rip out a man's heart, so this killer was no kingdom faerie. The humans could not cope with what he would bring. Even she did not know if she could do it alone. She would need help. Yet asking for help from the kingdom that threatened her life did not hold any appeal.

She considered this Munro and wondered how developed his power was, if indeed he had any. He didn't look like her mental image of a true druid, but she knew better than to judge too much on appearances. Humans aged quickly. As a young adult faerie, she was older than all living humans.

Eilidh climbed to an exposed beam within the second level of the empty, rotting church and made herself comfortable. The police still worked outside, and their voices filtered through the boarded-up lower windows. Their methods did not concern her. Once they departed, she would look for all the things they'd been incapable of seeing with human eyes.

CHAPTER 3

THE LONGEST DAY OF THE YEAR approached, so the sun rose early, a full three hours before the shops would open. This left Eilidh plenty of time. She stretched and made her way to the roof of St Paul's, using the loose flap on a boarded-up window to exit into the gloom. Lifeless grey clouds hung low and dulled the glow of the summer sun. Light mist fell, making the mossy stone ledges slick.

Eilidh glanced up and down the street and to the buildings around her before she made her way to the pavement below. Years ago, she'd cast a light warding around the church so that most humans didn't notice it. She was not a strong spell-caster, so it could not put off those determined to see. Rain had fallen through the night and washed away much, but not all, of the blood on the cobbled stones behind the church.

She crouched over the spot where the human had lain and opened her senses. When he'd first fallen, she'd been so concerned with the faerie and the blood shadows he'd cast that she hadn't paid attention to the victim. Now she wondered, *why this man?* A woman had walked with him. Eilidh distinctly remembered them passing below. They'd walked up together, then a few others had passed, and then the man had come back this way alone.

Having watched for so many years, Eilidh recognised some human habits. Women rarely travelled alone at night, except in groups. So the man had been escorting her either to her home or perhaps to a car.

Eilidh recalled their smells with sudden clarity. She'd noticed a chemical perfume about the woman. Humans put different scents in their hair, under their arms, and sprayed it on their bodies. It made them easy to detect among the street smells of food and machines. Add to that the alcohol on their breath, and...Eilidh stopped mid-thought. The woman had smelled of all of those things, but the man had not. She noticed it when he'd returned alone. The woman's scent clung to him in a faint, familiar way, but she wouldn't have even noticed him if she hadn't heard him. He smelled natural: no perfumes, no smoke, no alcohol. The more she thought about it, the stranger it seemed.

After the night's weather, it would be impossible to pick up even a faint trail, but Eilidh tried. She could smell nothing but the acidity of the street overlaid with the pleasant wafting sweetness that came with summer rain. She paused, bracing herself to do something she didn't like to do. She would not cast the azure—she would simply listen. The forbidden astral magic welled easily, pooling in her mind. Her thoughts opened, and suddenly she could see herself from above. With god-like eyes, she scanned the street below, aching with the details of every pore in the stone, each fleck of moss in every tiny crevice. Blood and death flooded her senses, and she could almost feel the life in those diluted cells that crept away with each tumbling raindrop. Larger forms of life: a white moth, a heather beetle, a small brown spider, a cluster of rats, birds flapping overhead, the force of their tiny existence beat loudly in her enhanced hearing.

Overwhelmed by the sensations, Eilidh fought to come back into her own mind, but her inexperience with the astral flows left her unable to control the power that thudded in her body. Even as she fought with herself, she recognised in a flash what was missing from the spot where the man's body had fallen. The knowing came before the words, but as the words formed in her mind, something else intruded.

Outcast. The word shuddered through her entire existence, relentlessly pressing in her ears. *Outcast.* He called to her, and Eilidh's mind was wide open because of the unpractised astral casting. The word echoed, beckoning and holding her as though he knew her past, future, and every intimate thought. How could one of the blood touch her thoughts? The realm of a blood faerie was flesh and bone, while an astral faerie touched perception, memory and illusion. Eilidh knew she should fight it, but her body was heavy and her magic wrapped in the miasma of her heightened senses.

She didn't have to ask who it was. Only a powerful faerie could do this. While she could have pretended it was one of her own kingdom come to redeem her, she didn't waste time on such hopes. Besides, she could taste the tang of blood magic in her mouth. None of the kingdom knew those rites.

Eilidh fell to the wet paving stones. She heard voices and felt the rough touch of human hands on her arms and throat. She smelled their breath. Their words came loudly, but the meanings took longer to take hold in her throbbing mind.

"You're okay." The voice soothed her and a part of her relaxed.

He had gone, no longer picking at the edges of her thoughts.

Eilidh opened her eyes and met the worried expression in his, which were a dark shade of blue. "Munro," she whispered. Her thoughts were now her own. She sighed. Her mind calmed, and she realised what was missing from the murder scene. Still looking intently at Munro, willing him to understand, she said, "The death occurred here. The casting of blood continued elsewhere." The words felt strange within her mouth, and she realised how long it had been since she had talked to someone else. English, of course, was not her native tongue. It had been spoken by humans in this land all her life, so she'd been taught. She also knew the tongues of the fae, Picts, Gaels, Swedes, and Celts, as well as Latin, even though she'd been born many hundreds of years after the Romans had come and gone from this island.

She struggled to sit up. Munro searched her eyes, seeming puzzled. Had she said something wrong? English had changed in her lifetime.

"You need to lie back, Miss. You've taken a tumble. An ambulance is on the way." To a few people crowding around, he said, "Give her some room to breathe. She'll be just fine."

Eilidh reached up behind her head and tugged at her hood to make sure it covered her ears. Munro stared into her eyes, investigating their strange colour, drifting in the swirls. Even for a faerie, Eilidh's eyes were remarkable.

A screeching siren approached. She could not let herself be taken. "Thank you, Munro," she said, twisting the English words in her mouth. He crouched beside her and looked up as the vehicle turned onto the nearby side street.

Eilidh's mind was weary from her encounter with the blood faerie, but her body was able. As soon as Munro's attention moved away, she sprang to her feet and darted south, dashing through traffic. She narrowly avoided a passing car, and she cursed. Normally, her perception would allow her to flit through the moving cars before drivers saw her. Today she felt like a lumbering cow. A sounding horn startled her.

She ran down Canal Street until she came to the River Tay. Without glancing back to see if she was being pursued, she ran to the water's edge and dove into the tidal river. Although in earth magic, her season was the first, and air her primary element, she also had some small influence with the second.

She allowed herself to feel the natural flows of the cold water. Without coming up for air, she let it carry her the short distance to the far side of Moncrieff Island and downriver, away from the city.

Recent rains made the swollen river flow swiftly to the east, so it took less than half an hour for Eilidh to reach the place where she intended to cross into fae territory. The cold Highland melt mixed with rainwater, and by the time Eilidh emerged from the river, she felt restored from her contact with the blood faerie. It disturbed her that she'd come so close to the humans. In twenty-five years, she'd managed to speak to them only on a handful of occasions. Most of those were in the early days before she'd grown accustomed to being alone.

Although she was not particularly strong in any of the Ways of Earth, fire was Eilidh's weakest element, so she opted for a simple spell of air magic. Her white hair danced on end as a gust of wind swirled around her, blowing frigid air over her clothes to dry them.

She sat on the bank of the river and took off her leather shoes. Still damp, she laid them aside and stared at the flowing water. She recalled the times when she and Saor had snuck away from their home boundaries and swum in the moonlight. It hadn't been too far from this spot. Using a shameful amount of effort, she mustered a little heat into a whirlwind she held in her hand.

Rather than continue, she decided to leave her garments slightly damp. It would be a mistake to approach the ever-fluxing kingdom boundaries at night. That was when the borders would come closest to the city. The Watchers would be more awake and better able to see her. No, she would do well to travel further, and meet the barriers when they were weakest. She should not delay.

Eilidh turned toward the hills and ran, fighting the fatigue that came from being awake in the middle of the day. She'd shaken off her earlier encounter and felt more herself with every step toward her former kingdom. She came upon long dirt roads that led through plastic-tented berry fields. Without missing a beat, she ran through them, not even bothering to shield her presence from the hunched field workers. Early on, she'd spent a great deal of energy trying to conceal her presence from the humans. That was before she'd realised they rarely paid attention.

Beyond the farms lay wide fields, separated by centuries-old stone dykes. Eilidh easily jumped the walls and dodged the sheep dotting the landscape. They scurried away as she ran, forcing her to acknowledge that she did not move as silently as her early training had required. A quarter of a century wasn't long, not when her people often lived for more than a millennium, but long enough for her to become careless and loud-footed.

When she finally came to the forest's edge, Eilidh hesitated. Once she stepped beyond this tree line, her life was forfeit. She might be able to find Saor, her childhood friend. They had often worked together in this very spot. They'd taken lessons together, played together, and when they approached adulthood, they'd trained and become

Watchers together. Everyone assumed they would marry, but before Eilidh reached the requisite century mark, she'd been exiled. When they arrested her, he'd not come to see her. She'd never gotten the chance to say goodbye.

Eilidh held up her hand and touched the nearest tree. Why was she here? Was it really to warn her people about the blood faerie she'd encountered? Now she was no longer certain what had kept her feet running in this direction. If she did encounter Saor, he would be forced to either kill her or help her.

She shook her head and smirked at her own foolishness. Saor would kill her or he wouldn't, but he was no longer hers. He would be close to a hundred and thirty, and if he hadn't found someone else by now, she'd be shocked. Even to suspect that he would not have taken another was ridiculous. He would have grieved, but when he found out about Eilidh's true nature, he would have counted himself lucky to escape her fate. As her childhood friend, no one would blame him for her crimes. If he'd been married to her though, the taint of her existence would never have left him.

A light breeze pushed at her back, and Eilidh steeled herself for whatever would come. With as much courage as she could muster, she stepped into the woods.

∞

Munro didn't mind house-to-house enquiries, generally speaking, especially not when someone like Gladys Pentworth offered him and Getty tea and freshly baked bread. Nobody made bread at home any more, except, it seemed, Gladys Pentworth. Munro and Getty sat on her beige settee to ask her, as they had most of her neighbours, if she saw or heard someone rip Robert Dewer's heart from his chest.

"Mrs Pentworth, were you home last night?"

"Why, yes, that poor felly." Her eyes widened with sympathy and she tutted. "Jam for your bread, dears?"

"No, madam, this is just fine. Did you know Robert Dewer?"

"No, no. I don't really keep up with young people anymore with their iPods and hoodies. The way they wear their trousers! Really, officers, can't anything be done?"

Getty coughed, and Munro schooled his features as best he could.

"Would you like some more tea?" she said to Getty, who hacked as though some bread had gone down the wrong way.

"Did you see or hear anything unusual last night?" Munro asked.

"Well, I heard him die. A horrible sound. He shrieked, the poor man. Didn't sound human." Her eyes were wide as though she could still hear it. Then she came back to the present moment, turning her head to the side and waiting for the next question.

Both officers sat forward. "You're sure it was him and not something off the telly?" Getty asked.

She frowned. "Really, you'd know a sound like that. Besides, I don't watch violent shows." She paused. "There's always foul noises coming from the street, you understand. This used to be a nice neighbourhood. At first I thought it was someone being sick. Then I thought that wasn't quite right either, was it?"

"What time was this?" Munro asked.

"Oh, must have been just before ten. I usually go to bed around then, see, and I had just cleaned my teeth."

"And what did you do then?"

"Well, I went to the window to see what the matter was. He was lying down there all alone. Sad, really, to die alone."

"You could see him from here?" Munro put his teacup on the coffee table and went to the window. He had to lean close to make out the church steps. The position of the building made it awkward.

"I couldn't see the body exactly, but I knew he had to be dead."

Munro turned back toward Mrs Pentworth and waited.

"Because of the angel, you see."

"Angel?" Munro and Getty glanced at each other.

"Yes, floated down from heaven. Just right after he died." She shook her head again.

Munro turned back to the window and peered up. He saw nothing but the church and the buildings opposite. St Paul's Street, the tiny, crowded road that curved behind the church, barely had room for a car to park. "Are you saying someone jumped down from one of those apartments?"

Her teacup rattled on the saucer when she set it down. "Don't be ridiculous. They'd have broken their neck. And no, they didn't come from the apartments." She narrowed her eyes. "It was an angel from heaven, come to take that poor Mr Dewer away. It didn't jump. Angels don't jump. It floated. And second, it came from heaven. I saw it descend from the sky."

"Yeah," Getty said with a glance to Munro. "If you think of anything more, give us a call." He handed her a card with the relevant phone numbers.

"Thank you," Munro said, and they left Mrs Pentworth to undoubtedly call her friends and report on the excitement.

After they made their way to the ground floor Getty said, "Nice old crackpot. Good bread. Shame she's such a loon."

"Maybe not," Munro said.

Getty stopped at the street exit. "I'm all for believing in the Good Lord when it comes to weddings and football, but don't tell me you believe she saw an angel."

Munro shook his head. "She saw something." Once on the street again, he glanced up at the grey sky. "I saw our witness this morning." He hadn't mentioned that he'd seen the girl, or that it *was* a girl. Her appearance left him unsettled, and he didn't want to admit that.

"The kid?"

"Short light hair, hazel eyes, maybe fifteen or sixteen? Foreign, I think. Hard to tell. Had some sort of medical condition. Collapsed on the steps. I only turned away for a second, and he stood up and ran off." Why was he still deceiving Getty? Munro could always claim later he hadn't realised. The girl certainly didn't seem ordinary. It would be an easy mistake for anyone to make.

"If he has a medical condition, he might be registered with a local GP. You think he's involved?"

"I think he's scared. Maybe he saw something, or maybe he's just scared of cops in general. You know how it is."

Getty nodded. Some families raised their kids to distrust the police. Usually it meant their mum was selling drugs out of their front room to make ends meet until dad got out of jail. One day on the outside and the old man would take up the family business again.

Munro also didn't tell Getty the girl hadn't been blonde. Her hair was white. Bright white, like his gran's, but without the blue tinge. And her silver-green eyes weren't like anything he'd seen. He couldn't get her face out of his mind. Something about her made him uneasy. He didn't like to think she was involved, but they had to find her, even if it was for her own protection. She seemed frail and small, but even though he'd told Getty she was a kid, he knew that wasn't right either.

Munro couldn't help but wonder about the angel Mrs Pentworth swore she'd seen. His hunches were stirring again, and he wished they'd just shut the hell up.

CHAPTER 4

"REALLY, CRIDHE, you're becoming quite mad."

Cridhe inclined his head as though deferentially agreeing with his father, but inside he seethed. The fae did not *go mad*. Dudlach should know that. Why would he suggest something so blatantly insulting to their race? Furthermore, Cridhe wasn't just any faerie. He was the hunter, vital to the Krostach Ritual because of his unique talents. When those with higher magic once again ruled the kingdoms, he would surely be made a lord. He was eccentric, perhaps. Driven, certainly. But never *mad*. "I enjoy my work," Cridhe said finally.

Dudlach's dark eyes flashed. "Too much, I think."

Impatience nipped at Cridhe. "Would you prefer I were timid and weak? Or have you simply developed an affinity for the human creatures?"

"Don't be disgusting. You always were a petulant child."

Cridhe held himself in a perfect calm pose, ignoring the roiling voices as best he could. "My point, Dudlach, is that I do a job that must be done. I enjoy it." Cridhe shrugged, as though the conversation bored him, but his mind ticked over every recent conversation he'd had with Dudlach, searching for signs of betrayal. "Is it wrong to find pleasure in service?"

"I have lived much longer than you," Dudlach said.

Cridhe bit back his internal response. Simply growing old was no accomplishment. Besides, Dudlach was dead. Somewhere in his twisted mind, Cridhe knew this, even if the ghost before him didn't. "Yes, that is so."

Was Dudlach a ghost? Cridhe didn't know. His mind wouldn't let him focus on the truth. He couldn't even ponder *why* he couldn't think about it.

"The higher magic should only be touched when necessary," his father said. "It is addictive, consuming. Blood magic even more so than the other three forms. You practice too much, draw too much."

For a moment, Cridhe forgot his concerns about Dudlach's state of being and launched into a familiar argument. "My drawing feeds the source stone. Without me…" Cridhe let the words trail off. They needed the sacrifices, and he alone could make them. He could not bear to be lectured by a shadow of a memory.

"Yes, what would we do without you?" Dudlach's eyes were so dark and the pupils so large it was impossible for Cridhe to tell if Dudlach was actually looking at him—or right through him.

His father's all-knowing air annoyed Cridhe. The old faerie was arrogant. And useless if he wouldn't practice or teach more of what he knew of blood magic.

"Cridhe!" Dudlach's voice made him jump. "You're muttering to yourself again. This is what I mean. This is what worries me."

"Was I?" A tinge of doubt crept into Cridhe's mind. He forced a weak smile. "I'm overtired, perhaps. Nothing more."

A cloud moved through Dudlach's eyes. "Rest, then. Our work is vital."

Dudlach stalked into the surrounding trees. Cridhe watched the blackness intently. When Cridhe had killed Dudlach, he'd tasted the magic, consumed it, but it had not become part of him. It ran through him, as would any meat. He'd tried to collect Dudlach's heart the same way he now did with humans, but it hadn't worked. The spell failed and the heart ceased its beating. In many ways, it hadn't entirely surprised him. The fae, being superior to lower life forms, were far too complex to have the same weaknesses as humans.

A flicker of recognition threatened, but Cridhe denied the horror he should have felt at having killed his own father. Dudlach had deserved to die.

∞

Munro squinted out the window into the bright afternoon. His eyes resisted, and he had to lower them again. The light burned. He'd never had a migraine before, but he'd known plenty of people who had, so he wondered if that was what he was experiencing. Migraine sufferers never seemed to miss an opportunity to describe, in excruciating detail, why theirs was no ordinary headache.

"You all right?" Getty asked. He said it with a chuckle, as though he only asked out of social convention.

Munro never got sick, took a sick day, or so much as had a cold. "Yeah," he said. "Just a bit of a bad head."

Sergeant Hallward happened to be walking through the squad room. "Shake it off, cupcake. We have work to do," he said without even breaking stride.

Munro chuckled. "Yes, boss." But Hallward was already out of earshot by the time the words had come. He turned to ask Getty if he wanted to grab some lunch before the St Paul's case review, but suddenly he found his face planted in the dark grey carpet.

"Jesus," Getty said, kneeling beside his partner.

Munro felt himself being rolled over and then Getty's cool hand touching his face. Munro tried to speak, but vomit sprayed out of his mouth, all over Getty's black uniform and onto the shoes of nearby officers.

"We need an ambulance at Divisional Police Headquarters on Barrack Street..."

Why did they use such a strange monotone when talking to dispatch? Why did everyone sound so worried? Had the killer struck again?

Munro wasn't surprised at the thought. The killing had been so bizarre. Someone who could do something like that to a person wouldn't hesitate to do it again. Unnecessary violence would usually indicate that a killing had been personal. In this case, it hadn't been so much violent as just bloody wrong. Munro had heard one young idiot breathe the phrase "serial killer" when Hallward had been within earshot. It hadn't taken very many words to shut the kid up. Serial meant more than one, a pattern, a predator. Right now, they had one dead bloke and one sick killer.

Anyone would know why you didn't say things like that before you had to. Just the idea of a serial killer in Perth made Munro's stomach tighten. Perth was his city. He'd been born here, gone to school here, and becoming a copper had been the most natural thing in the world. Some people dreamed of moving away, going to university in Edinburgh or Glasgow, maybe even London. One mate had gone to America, for pity's sake. He'd gotten an athletic scholarship to a university in a state Munro couldn't have found on a map. Ohio or Oregon or something. But Munro knew Scotland was where he belonged. He wasn't settling; he was home.

The thoughts drifted through Munro's mind. He felt oddly calm and removed as though he could finally think clearly, separated from his physical reality.

Someone placed a plastic mask over Munro's face. The cool air smelled strange, as though it were too clean, too pure...the smell of nothing. Something jostled Munro. He felt movement and heard voices, calm, but no-nonsense. He used that tone sometimes himself. Cops learned quickly how to talk without leaving room for argument or negotiation. Some people needed help focusing. Usually if anyone needed a cop, there was something bad happening. He had to talk to people who were distressed, angry, grieving, or clouded by alcohol or drugs. Clear, crisp commands. That was the only thing that would get through. *Step away now* or *get out of the vehicle, please* or *I'm sorry. There's been an accident.*

Clear and calm. That's what Getty sounded like when he said, "I'm right here, Munro. We're almost there. Don't worry."

Munro wanted to take him aside. Don't tell people what *not* to do. Tell them what to do. Always issue commands in the positive. If a cop says, "Don't worry," all they hear is the word *worry*.

A hard pain hit Munro's spine as it lurched into an awkward curve, arching his back off the surface where he lay. Muscles contracted, jerking and releasing, jerking and releasing. The calm voices grew insistent and frenzied, but in a controlled, orchestrated way.

Swirling colours turned black, and all sound grew distant.

Munro floated for a while. The blackness became grey and vague. The pain had evaporated, and the voices stilled. He loved the silence. Some people filled their heads with music or flicked on the telly for company, but Munro found comfort in quiet. This particular silence was more complete than any he'd ever experienced. He felt as if he were wrapped in a cloud, miles away from even the most distant traffic or the slightest breeze.

He saw mottled green. Then he saw *her*. She walked through the woods, moving away from him. He recognised the spiky white hair. He couldn't help but marvel at the economy of her movements as she navigated the dense, uneven forest. He followed, floating behind her without gaining ground. Once, she stopped. He almost felt her listening. She lifted her face, and her head twitched to the side. Was she sniffing the air? Suddenly, she whipped her head around and looked right at him. Part of him flinched, but when he saw her puzzled expression, he realised she couldn't see him. That was when he noticed the gentle, corkscrew turn at the top of her ears. Her swirling eyes scanned the woods behind her. Her body poised with the tension of a wild animal, ready to pounce—or to flee. *So beautiful*, he thought. As he voiced the words, she faded away, and his world returned to blackness.

CHAPTER 5

THE PECULIAR SENSATION of eyes prickling against her skin made Eilidh glance over her shoulder. It shouldn't surprise her. She had been a Watcher, but it didn't take long away from the kingdom to lose the sharpness of her skills. She had spent nearly a quarter of her life in exile. A twinge of sadness and longing threatened to surface, and she pushed it back to the recesses of her mind. Self-pity would wait. For now, she had to focus on a greater purpose. It pleased her to have one after so long of merely surviving.

"You smell like a human." The voice floated to her as a whisper on the wind.

Her heart lurched. "Saor." She stepped away from the tree, so she could be clearly seen from all sides, and opened her mouth slowly to show she held no incantations.

"Your life is forfeit in the kingdom," he said, approaching her from the trees. His long golden hair hung straight around his pale face and shone in the morning light. His dark grey eyes appeared hard and unwavering—like the stone magic he favoured. Eilidh could not read them.

"Yes." Now was the moment, she thought. He would either kill her or not. He'd loved her once, but did he love duty more?

Suddenly, he stood in front of her. It startled Eilidh. His skills had grown over the past decades while hers dulled.

"So you have come to die?" His angry, mocking tone shocked Eilidh. This was not the Saor she remembered.

"I bring news to the conclave." She licked her lips, feeling more nervous than she had expected. When she decided to warn them of the deaths and report that one of the forbidden, higher forms had been used, it made sense at the time. Any of their kingdom would have done the same. Now, standing and facing the one who would have been her mate, she realised her folly. She wasn't a kingdom faerie any longer. Had she been sitting in that tower all those long years waiting for an excuse to come back? *Fool.* She'd convinced herself she'd accepted her fate, but seeing the disgust on Saor's beautiful face made her heart ache with renewed pain.

He stepped back and flicked his eyes to the trees as though pondering her words. His hesitation lasted only a moment. "What news?"

"Someone has cast blood shadows in the city."

His eyes turned sharp again, cutting her with accusation.

"Not me, Saor. You know my crimes were in the astral realm, not the blood."

His perfectly angled features froze, as though he did not even breathe. They had never once spoken of her wrongdoing. But then, he'd never come to see her after the truth became known, nor even sent word. Finally, Saor gave a barely perceptible nod.

"He killed a human."

Saor snorted his lack of concern. "Does this bother you?"

Eilidh winced at his derisive manner. "It was brutal. Violent. And yet controlled and purposeful." She turned her chin up to stare Saor squarely in the face. "Powerful."

Saor narrowed his eyes, calculating again. He had not, Eilidh thought, been so stoic and hard before. Had she done this? Was he yet another casualty of her deformed magical talents? They used to laugh together, all those many years ago. Now, seeing his stony expression, she couldn't remember what his laughter sounded like.

"Do you know who he is? Has another been exiled since my...departure?"

"Since you tried to kill your own father and ran away?"

Another blow to the heart. "He lives then?"

Saor nodded. "He told the conclave that he fell and said when he awoke, you had gone. An obvious lie."

Eilidh did not let herself smile, but she was pleased by her father's cleverness. If he'd told the story of her overpowering him, they might have suspected him. But since he told them the opposite, they blamed her instead.

"Too obvious," Saor said, a warning in his tone.

He knew. And he was telling her, as clearly as any faerie would speak. Was there threat in his words? If anyone learned that her father helped her escape, he could face the same fate. "What do you want, Saor?"

He blinked at her directness. It was not their way. The fae spoke in half-nods and flicks of the eyes. "You have changed, Eilidh."

She fought the bitterness in her throat. "The human world is ugly, Saor, and I have grown slow. I miss..." Eilidh could not say it. She would not let herself reminisce about the Halls of Mist or the Otherworld. Only the outer reaches of the fae kingdoms overlapped the human plane. Even they were forbidden to her.

The pair stood in long silence. Another thing Eilidh missed. Humans rushed everywhere, filled every moment with noise. They lacked the discipline of quiet.

Finally, Eilidh spoke again. "This blood faerie. He smells *wrong*, Saor. And strong. I tracked him, but the trail vanished." She wondered if she should tell him that the faerie had touched her mind but decided that would only remind Saor of her own wrongness.

"I've never known you to lose a trail."

She nodded her appreciation of the compliment. "Do you know who he is?" she asked again. Few of the fae would choose to live outside the kingdoms. The pull of the Otherworld was too strong.

Saor turned his face downward to indicate he did not, a subtle gesture that made her smile. Even with the horrible and irreparable rift between them, she had missed him. It pleased her to see she still recognised his tiniest movements.

"If he attacks again, could you best him?"

Eilidh had wondered that herself, but only briefly. "No. You know me, Saor. I've never been strong."

"Not in the Ways of Earth, no."

His admission surprised her. Earth magic was the only acceptable magic among the fae. She'd been weak, ridiculously so. Like the runt of a litter, expected to crawl away and die because the Mother Earth had rejected her. It had always been Saor who protected her, he who trained her in the skills of the Watchers. What she lacked in magical talent, he taught her tenfold in plant lore, agility, strength, and skill. And now he spoke to her of the Path of the Azure, forbidden to the fae because of its corruptive and addictive nature.

"I had no training in astral magic."

He knew as well as she that her statement, although true, did not answer his question.

She relented. "No. I could not best him with the Path of the Azure. I resist the flows, so they are unfamiliar to me."

"You keep the law?"

His surprise annoyed Eilidh. "I am fae," she said.

"You are not of our kingdom," he reminded her.

"I am fae," she repeated, setting her jaw firmly.

A flicker of a smile passed his lips and then disappeared. "I will speak to the conclave. I doubt they will trouble themselves, but they will want to know of this...turn."

"Thank you," she said, feeling bereft as she realised their conversation had drawn to a close. "Will you tell my father I am well?"

"Would it be true?"

"Will you tell him?"

She thought she saw a nod, but his movement was so faint and her senses so dulled from exile, she couldn't be certain.

All trace of tenderness or friendship left Saor's features. His eyes grew hard, as though he suddenly remembered what she had become. "Go, Eilidh. Your life is forfeit if you stay here." In a blur, Saor touched her cheek before disappearing into the trees. The rocks at her feet vibrated as he cast his words into the stone. "Go," they said.

No longer able to stand the memories of what she had lost forever, Eilidh turned and ran.

∞

Munro didn't remember deciding to go into the woods. He tried not to think about it, because he didn't remember how he got there. All he knew was that something was *missing*. Confused and feverish, he wasn't entirely sure what it was missing *from*.

He did recall waking up in the hospital. Someone had taken off his stab-vest and utility belt, but he still wore his uniform when he woke up in A&E. He'd heard Getty telling someone that Munro had questioned a witness who'd had some kind of seizure. The doctors had instructed Getty not to worry. His partner was in good hands, they'd said.

Those good hands came by and took blood, checked his temperature and blood pressure, and wrote on charts. Nurses asked him questions for which he could make no coherent answer. He felt as though he'd been drugged. His words slurred and his vision warped like he was floating under water. The clearest thing in his mind was *her*. The way she looked at him pierced his clouded mind.

"Ears," he said. They were so cute, the way they curled at the top, but those eyes made him take her *very* seriously. Beautiful, yes. Delightful and enchanting, definitely. But absolutely dangerous. He hoped and prayed she wasn't involved in the murder at St Paul's. He knew better than to fool himself. She wasn't some innocent waif.

A face appeared in front of him. "Do your ears hurt, Mr Munro?"

"Twisted," he replied, exhausted from the effort.

"All right then, pet. I'll tell the doctor," she said. In a quieter voice, as though speaking to someone on the other side of the room, she added, "'Twisted,' he said. His fever isn't coming down." She tutted, and Munro felt the curtained cubicle empty.

The Accident and Emergency department was never completely silent. He'd been here plenty of times to take accident reports, interview victims, respond to reports about stab injuries and the rare gunshot wound. Long ago, he'd come when his dad fell ill with cancer. He pushed that unwelcome memory aside.

Munro opened his eyes. He felt strange, but at least he could focus. He was, as he had suspected, alone. His eyes turned to the east. Beyond the hospital and the city and the river, it was there. Something called him. It wasn't her that called, but whatever it was, it drew him. He had to find out who she was, what she was, and...then what? He didn't know. His mind would surely clear by the time he got there.

Getty must have taken his stab-vest and utility belt, because they weren't in the cubicle, but that was okay. Munro checked his pockets. He had his wallet, keys, and his shoes. They hadn't had the time to get him properly undressed and into a hospital bed. If he didn't hurry, they'd be back to do just that.

He didn't have any trouble getting out of the hospital. No one thought to stop a cop from doing anything. One of the benefits of his job was that people saw the uniform, not the face. He reached the doors before he heard someone behind him say, "Have you seen the policeman who was here a moment ago?"

Outside, it took a minute to get his bearings. He walked down the hill toward the car parks, going right past the buses, down Rose Crescent and toward the Queen's Bridge. Along the way, things got hazy. He quit thinking about walking—quit thinking about anything. He just moved, closer and closer to...something.

She could help him. Of that he had no doubt. The closer he got, the better he felt. For once he wasn't planning and carefully deciding. He just walked.

After a long while, Munro stumbled. How long had he been out here? The memory of his journey was dim. His legs shook. He felt hungry and exhausted. He wanted to lie in the cool grass. It took a moment to get his bearings. Tall green trees surrounded him. A tractor growled far in the distance, so he thought he was somewhere near a farm. The ground did look comfortable. *Why was he here?* He couldn't remember. Maybe if he sat down and took a moment to consider, everything would make sense later. He only needed a rest.

∞

It didn't take long for Eilidh to reach the border of the kingdom lands. They weren't marked by sign or stone, or even cutting river or stone dyke. Unlike human borders, the influence of the kingdom lands moved like the tides, spreading out at night when the fae were at their most powerful and receding in the light of day.

Passing outside the kingdom lifted danger from her shoulders. The fae would not come after her in the human world. She posed no threat as long as she stayed away. Even still, she felt bereft all over again. Every part of her wanted to run back to Saor, beg his forgiveness, tell him it had been a horrible mistake. But she couldn't. The fae conclave was not known for reasonableness. Her exile hadn't arisen from her actions, although she had committed criminal acts, but from her existence. She could touch forbidden magic. The mere ability made her an outlaw.

The moment she stepped outside the barrier, she felt a presence. Someone sought her. Something in the unrelenting focus on her created a small but constant mental pressure point she could not ignore. Questions filled her mind. The magic was like none she had encountered before. It felt strange and foreign. It sparked curiosity and fear. Fae magic always felt familiar, even if she did not know the incantation or the one who cast it.

The source, she felt certain, came from some distance. She could possibly avoid it by going far west and then doubling back to Perth. It would take time, because she would have to travel in an odd meandering line to avoid the kingdom territories that stretched hundreds of miles. Human clusters burned holes in the fae's influence and protection. At this time of year, with the long summer days, she had more breathing room than usual. But there were many pockets of strength she must avoid at all costs. Few would show as much compassion as Saor if she were discovered.

Curiosity and...something else...made her squint toward the distant source of alien magic. It drew her. She stopped dead in the forest, frozen so completely that her muscles complained. Eilidh forced herself to relax and take one step after another toward the source of this peculiar sensation. A faint wish for her father's advice flitted through her mind. She pushed it away with a barely-breathed curse. She had to learn to think differently. Wishing for her old life made her worse than foolish.

The foreign magic tugged, and she moved more steadily toward it. She was fae. What could she have to fear? The question taunted her, but she ignored the well-practiced jibes. *Faith*. She was fae.

After more than an hour of walking, she could nearly touch the aura of the strange magic. She circled around and listened. She felt a presence, but only one. She heard no speech. The wind, with some gentle coaxing, brought the scent of a human, definitely male. Her old skills as a Watcher came quickly back. She climbed up a sturdy conifer. Humans rarely glanced up. The source did not move, but it did pulse. She wished, not for the first time, that she had not been born so utterly incompetent in the stone element. Then she could have spoken to the ground beneath his feet.

He stirred. Climbing down, she inched closer, staying well hidden, unable to resist his pull. *Munro.* Fear tingled in her skin. What *was* he?

When she stepped into the clearing where he lay nestled in a bed of pine needles, his eyes fluttered. He gazed at her, his eyes burning with delirium and said the last word she would have expected. "*Dem'ontar-che.*" Love, in the ancient fae language.

Yet more than love. Devotion didn't even define it. The phrase was spoken only at sacred ceremonies, and never lightly. It implied blind faith, utter servitude, and unquestioning loyalty.

Eilidh's eyes widened. "What did you say?"

Munro blinked his red, bleary eyes and slowly sat up. He shook his head, as though trying to clear it. His keen eyes took in the clearing and then fastened on her. "How did I get here?"

"Munro," she persisted. "What did you say to me?"

He rubbed his hands over his face and paused a moment before struggling to rise. Eilidh could see he was stalling, working his thoughts, trying to remember.

"'Damn, my arse,' I think it was." He grinned in a half-hearted apology. He looked around the forest again. "How did you find me?"

Eilidh reached toward him, running her fingers over the magic that pulsed between them. "I think you found me."

He moved toward her, and it took all her will not to step away. *I am fae*, she reminded herself.

His hand went to the side of her face and traced the gentle curve of her upturned ear. "I thought it was a fevered dream," he said. Eilidh tried to pull her hood up, but Munro pushed it back. "No, don't. Please. I want to see." With a fingertip he touched her ear and stared at her spiky white hair before settling his gaze on her eyes. "Where are you from?" he finally asked.

Eilidh started to turn away, but his hand guided her face back to meet his gaze. "Here," she said. He clearly had no idea what an intimate gesture he'd made.

Munro chuckled. "That's no Perth accent you've got."

A century of teaching railed against her. *Avoid the humans. Never speak to them. Whatever you do, never reveal our existence. They would seek us out and destroy us. We are stronger individually, but they have numbers and machines. They would drive us into the Otherworld completely, and we would be forced to shut our gates to the Ways of Earth forever.*

Eilidh saw that he understood. The frown that quickly replaced the smile told her he had likely worked it out. Perhaps he only wanted confirmation that he had not gone completely mad.

After a very long, intense silence she said, "I am fae."

He sat, silently searching her face, as though he could read the truth in her expression. She felt him processing it, making a decision.

Although she didn't know why, she wanted to reassure him. She wanted him to believe her. Perhaps, more than anything, it occurred to her that maybe she didn't have to spend the rest of eternity alone. One person could know, perhaps. One friend. Maybe. This strange human shed a ray of hope into her life.

Eilidh suddenly glanced up. It had gotten late. "Faith," she cursed.

"What is it?" Munro said, turning as though listening to the forest around them.

"Darkness falls, and the gateway to the Otherworld will soon open." When Munro stared blankly, she explained further. "We must go. The kingdom borders are expanding."

It was more words than she had ever spoken to a human at one time. She didn't know how he would respond. She could, of course, leave him behind. He would be in less danger than she when the borders overtook them. The kingdom fae did not hunt men who did not seek trouble. But, inexplicably, she didn't want to. She wanted him to accept and follow her.

"Your eyes are shining," he said.

She nodded. "As darkness falls, I will be able to see much better than you. Take my hand." She offered her long, pale fingers, but he hesitated before accepting. When the skin of his palm engulfed hers, heat washed into her, racing up her arm. A wave of concern passed over her. Was he ill? She didn't worry about contracting a disease from him. The fae did not succumb to human ailments, but she searched his eyes. He did seem slightly red in the face, but she had no time to worry for him. She could not be found here once darkness fell. "Come, I will guide you to the city."

CHAPTER 6

I AM FAE, SHE had said.

Munro lay in his bed and replayed the scene. She'd led him by the hand. An old melody played in his head. *Over hill-way up and down...Myrtle green and bracken brown.* She'd guided him as far as the Old Bridge and scanned his face with those eyes like pools of liquid silver. When she appeared satisfied with what she saw, she let go.

He grabbed her wrist, and she flinched. Could she seriously be afraid of him? "What's your name?" he asked her.

She hesitated, as though giving her name would give away so much more. "Eilidh," she said. An odd name, old and rich in texture, but once he heard it, he couldn't imagine anything more right for her. Then she left him, running faster than she should have been able to. He watched until she slipped out of sight, but he couldn't help but notice that passers-by ignored her, as though she didn't register in their minds.

He must be losing it. Somewhere deep, he accepted her. His logical brain, on the other hand, told him to go straight back to the hospital. He was too tired to be reasonable, so he turned toward home. It only took a few minutes to walk to Mill Street, and from there get the bus to the Tulloch Institute a few blocks from his house. By the time he put his key in the front door, it was pitch dark. Only when he heard his landline ringing did he realise he must have lost his mobile sometime during the day.

He answered like always. "Munro."

No *hello* or *how are you* greeted him. "Jesus. Where have you been?" It was Getty. "The hospital said you walked out."

"Aye," Munro said, not sure how to explain himself. "A bit out of it, I guess. How's the St Paul's case going? Any word?"

Getty hesitated. "Not much, really. The victim, Robert Dewer, seems to have no enemies, no recent arguments, not much of a social life at all. The woman he was seen with at the bar, Alison Brice, said she just met him that night. He hadn't been acting strange, and nobody can see a reason anyone would want him dead."

"Damn," was all Munro said to that.

"Yeah."

So a real whodunit. No motive and no witnesses. Except Eilidh.

I am fae.

Munro didn't know what her presence or her race meant, in terms of their case, and it surprised him that he wanted to believe her strange pronouncement. But even he, a natural sceptic, reinforced by years of hearing every lie and excuse a man might invent, could not deny what he saw in Eilidh's eyes or heard in her voice—not to mention those ears. But a faerie? Could it possibly be?

"I'm back at the doc's in the morning. I'm hoping to get word that'll get me cleared for duty." He didn't mention that he'd spoken to the one possible witness to the murder. Not yet. He felt protective of her, even though he wasn't sure why. Munro's head hurt, and he knew none of this made any sense.

"Alright then," Getty said. His partner understood that he didn't want to be off work during the biggest investigation their careers would likely see.

"I'm going to bed. Been a long night. I'll ring you first thing."

They said goodbye and Munro did as he said he would. The day had utterly exhausted him. Had he really napped in the forest? He could almost believe his encounter with Eilidh had been nothing more than a fevered dream. Almost.

Although Munro had nearly talked himself out of returning to the hospital, he didn't get the chance to back out. Eight hours after that phone call, Getty banged on the door and offered him a lift, even though Munro lived less than a mile from the Perth Royal Infirmary.

They didn't have to wait long to see the doctor who'd ordered the blood tests the day before. The doc told Munro the tests were inconclusive— probably meaning they showed diddly—but the doctor wasn't happy about the seizure. He wanted Munro to get an MRI and didn't think they should put it off.

Munro knew an MRI wouldn't reveal anything either. He'd been sick and seen a vision of Eilidh. Somehow, he'd found her. Then when he did, he got better. He didn't believe in coincidence, but he wasn't daft enough to tell anyone he'd been seeing faeries. They'd have him in a hospital gown before he knew what happened—and possibly a padded room.

Getty offered to stay, but Munro knew that even though the doctor said he'd get him squeezed in that day, it would take a while. Munro went to get some coffee and begin a long day of trying not to think about the girl who turned his life upside down with three words: *I am fae.*

∞

Rather than returning to the church tower, Eilidh slept most of the day on Moncreiffe Island, the forty-six-hectare strip of golf course, garden allotments, and woodlands that divided an elbow of the River Tay into two channels. Because it was attached to the city by a footbridge and a rail line passed over, it was well beyond the influence of the fae kingdom, even at night when the borders expanded. The area was small, and the presence of foot-bound golfers and fishermen meant it didn't offer her much privacy, so Eilidh didn't dare make this a permanent haunt. However, it was less trafficked than the city's two large parks. Best of all, it was green. She could hide amongst the trees and brush and feel the power of the cool water on all sides. The previous night, Eilidh had felt the coursing magic of the kingdom air. After that, she hadn't been ready to surround herself with stone, rats, noise, and pollution. Not yet.

As the sun crossed the horizon, Eilidh shook herself awake. She'd taken the habits of humans, in some ways, sleeping at least occasionally at night, even though she felt less alert and weaker during the day. But after her meeting with Saor, she realised she'd been marking time. Now she forced herself to imagine a future. Would she continue to hide among humans for the centuries to come? Could she imagine integrating with them? Passing for one of them? The idea seemed ludicrous. What would she do?

Eilidh shook her head. These thoughts were foolish. She couldn't pass for a human any more than a shepherd could pass for a lamb. Besides, she had more important things to think about. Her thoughts went back to the killing at St Paul's, and the blood shadows that had been used as a weapon. Even if the conclave refused to take notice, she had to find out who'd slaughtered the man below the tower and why. She hadn't felt the blood faerie's voice again since she'd returned to Perth, but he couldn't be far away.

Eilidh. When she first heard it, she tensed, but then realised she'd only done so because the blood shadows had been on her mind. She recognised the voice carried on the wind. Saor arrived a few minutes later, just as dusk fell, looking magnificent and serene as he always did. She drank in the scent of Otherworld that wafted around him.

"You live here?" he asked as he stepped into the small clearing where she sat cross-legged, waiting for him. His eyes swept over the thin protection of the trees and shallow, barely perceptible flows of earth magic.

"No," she said. "This is much greener than the place I live, Saor." Her tone held a challenge. She did not need his condemnation or want his pity. Once, she had wanted his love, but that time had passed into dust. There was no point wanting things that could never be.

He nodded. "The conclave will do nothing," he said.

"You told them of the blood shadows, of the killing?"

Saor's keen eyes glistened in the darkness. "Of course. I left nothing out."

Eilidh hadn't realised until that moment how much she had counted on their help. She couldn't stop this unnatural magic on her own. "More will die," she said.

"You could go south, to the wastes. You could hide more easily there."

A cold dread clenched her stomach. Down into the concrete wastelands of Edinburgh and its ever-growing burn of technology? "What of this blood faerie? Shall I leave him then, to feed on the men of this city?"

Amusement filled Saor's eyes. "Are you their Watcher? They are many. Even humans know that when a herd is too large, it should be culled."

Eilidh thought of Munro, of his strange, alien, pulsing magic. "They are not so different from us as we might have once thought."

Saor did not answer. Instead, he watched Eilidh as the silence between them stretched on. Finally, he asked, "Why did you not tell me?"

It took Eilidh a long moment before she realised what he meant. Her forbidden talents. The reason behind her exile. Her tainted and twisted magical curse. "I was a child. I did not know." The weight of the memories dragged her into sadness. "Even if I had understood, it was better you did not."

A subtle flick of his head told her of his annoyance. "You think not?"

"If you knew I could cast the azure and said nothing, you would have been condemned alongside me."

"Or I could have helped you stop." He paused. "I always aided you, Eilidh."

She smiled at him now. "You did. But could you stop hearing the stone call to you? Could you sever yourself from the Ways of Earth?"

"Of course not," he said. "But the Ways of Earth are natural. Do you think the conclave would have forbidden the Path of the Azure without reason? Its magic is twisted and dangerous. Piedre should have been enough to prove that to you."

"I have paid for the wrong done to him." Eilidh avoided thinking about the young faerie whose life she nearly took with her accidental illusions. "I do not cast the azure. I told you that."

"Yet you say you could not sever yourself from it."

"I am what I am. My crime was being born."

"Self-pity does not suit you. You have grown thin of heart."

"And you are as self-congratulating as ever, Saor. Go. The Otherworld calls. I have not grown so thin that I cannot hear it."

"Will you go south?"

"No. This is my home. *These* are my people now. Maybe I am their Watcher." She was not certain she believed her own words, but saying them made her feel stronger. They gave her purpose after decades of mere existence.

Saor's face was still unreadable. He stood and turned to go. "Your father sends his blessings. He hopes you are well and happy. I told him you are."

"Thank you," Eilidh said. All three would know it for a lie. No faerie could be well or happy outside the kingdom. Could they? "Goodbye, Saor. Thank you for delivering my warning to the conclave, even if they chose to ignore it."

He responded with a curt nod and disappeared through the trees, heading north.

Eilidh stood and went west to the footbridge that connected the island to the city. She pulled her hood up to cover her hair and ears and walked aimlessly. She looked closely at the humans that stood at bus shelters or walked to pubs and restaurants. The night was still young. Cars with their cold, artificial eyes of light crept through the streets, carrying people to their homes. For the first time, Eilidh wondered what it would feel like to sit in the metal cage and be trundled down the road. She liked being on her feet, connected to the earth, but tonight she saw these people differently.

If they knew what she was, would they be frightened? Would they accept her? She thought of Munro. He seemed to be drawn to her. But then, he was something different too, perhaps as different from his people as she was from hers.

Eilidh stared at the stars, where her forbidden magic flowed. If she were to be the city's only Watcher, she would need all the help she could find. The conclave had turned their back on her, and she didn't know how to touch the magic flows above her. Always before, the astral magic flooded her without warning, overwhelming her senses. She had been taught that to touch the Path of the Azure was to tempt fate and the surest way to madness. It would mean risking death, but what was that to her now? She had no home, no family, no friends. She possessed nothing and owed no one. All she had was this place. She could let this blood faerie drive her further into the wastes, or she could take the chance to protect a city that did not even know her.

CHAPTER 7

CRIDHE HAD NOT DARED TO BREATHE when the Watcher called Saor approached the island. Although he knew the blood shadows were superior to the Ways of Earth, he had never tested his strength against a kingdom faerie. Dudlach raised him to fear the kingdom, while still speaking with wistful jealousy. As a child, Cridhe wanted to hear again and again about the Halls of Mist. His father indulged him for a time, but after a while, he told Cridhe to put his childish dreaming behind him. The pair lived beneath the notice of the kingdoms, but not for much longer.

A year ago, finding an exiled female who could walk the Path of the Azure would have been a gift of fate. After all, how could they seed a new kingdom without someone to bear the children? They had heard rumour of her existence, but never encountered her.

With their new plans, their need was not as urgent. Soon they would have their pick of the kingdom fae.

Still, discovering her held a promise. They would take the kingdoms back, and mating with another of the Path of the Azure would increase the chances of a purer, more elite bloodline. Dudlach had explained that if two with earth magic mated, the chance of a child with higher magic was one in a thousand. If one parent had talents in the Path, the chances raised to a third. With both though? The gifts were never assured, but the chances were doubled. The magic came from the child's own fate and manifested in a way as unique as a soul itself.

Cridhe pulled his thoughts to the present and focused his blood. He did not dare cast shadows, or the Watcher called Saor might see it. But he did envelop his own essence in pure darkness, a pocket of nothingness that would stand out only if Saor bathed the island in light.

The blood faerie listened to their conspiratorial conversation, staying perfectly still until Saor departed and Eilidh made her way into the city streets. Cridhe had learned several interesting things; foremost was the mention of the "crimes" for which Eilidh had been exiled. She had said, "I do not cast the azure." So she had skills of the Path, as he had known, but not of the blood. Dudlach had always called their talents "casting shadows," so hers must be astral, not of blood. The only other fae he had known followed the Path, but their talent was like his, drawing of flesh and bone. So, what could she do and how strong was she?

Cridhe had no choice. He had to ask Dudlach. He could do it subtly, so the elder faerie did not understand the meaning behind it. Something about that troubled him, but he couldn't place what. His mind teetered on the edge of recognition, but frustratingly, it was denied him.

Of course, Dudlach would know of the exile. Cridhe remembered Dudlach talking about the few fae who survived departing the kingdom. Yet even Dudlach, with all his wisdom, would not have expected her to stay so close to her family. Cridhe had been born hundreds of miles away, across the water, and yet here stayed Eilidh, within a whisper's breadth of her own people. If he had known, before he died, of course, Dudlach would have found her and claimed her, as he had Cridhe's mother. Maybe he tried when she first left the kingdom and never told Cridhe. It would be like his father to hide a failure. Or maybe he feared her azuri magic.

It was enough to give Cridhe pause. Oh, he would have her. With Eilidh feeding his talents, he could challenge the throne, make her the new Faerie Queen. The more he thought about it, the more he realised it had been his destiny all along.

He waited long enough for Eilidh to be well away from the footbridge, but not so long that he would have to swim ashore if she returned. Yes, she would be his, but not quite yet. Tonight he had more important business, something that would take him a step closer to the Halls of Mist.

∞

Munro lay on his couch, stared at the ceiling, and ignored the inane babble on the telly. The day at the hospital had felt like a week. At least they hadn't insisted on keeping him overnight. Sergeant Hallward had called and ordered Munro to do whatever the doctors told him. They would not, however, clear him to go back to work yet. A killer was out walking free—at the very least, a sick bastard, and at worst, a serial killer—and Munro had to stay home. There was nothing bloody wrong with him, and he had half a mind to tell Hallward that. Fortunately for him, the *other* half of his mind was reasonably sane. All he had to do was lie low for a couple of days while waiting for a few more useless lab results. Then, when nothing else happened, he could convince the occupational health advisor he was better off at work.

With a flick of the remote, he silenced the noise. He had to get moving. He'd never been the kind to enjoy lying around the house. It always sounded great, the idea of sleeping in, watching crap on the box, having nothing to do. But he just wasn't the type. When it came right down to it, Munro couldn't stand doing nothing.

Hauling himself up, he went to his exercise room. It had been intended by the builders, no doubt, to serve as a child's bedroom. It contained precisely three objects: a table, a stereo, and a treadmill. Munro wasn't a big collector of junk, and he kept the décor sparse. He liked things to serve a purpose, so he didn't fill his house with throw pillows and knick-knacks. His mum had loved her ornaments, as she called them, but when she died, his dad waited about a week before boxing them up and giving them to a charity shop. "I loved your mum,

Quinton," he'd said, "but I hate them fuckin' porcelain cats."

When his dad died of cancer many years later, Munro found the old man had already taken care of just about everything a person could. Considerate to the last, not wanting to be a burden to his only child. The old man's house sold quickly, leaving Munro enough cash to buy this place. It had three bedrooms, only one of which served as such. The second bedroom contained a desk, a dusty computer, and his camping gear.

Munro's feet pounded against the treadmill. He checked his watch and took his pulse. His heart rate was perfectly in the zone. He stared out the window and tried not to think about *her*. But trying not to think about her meant a keen awareness of avoiding her, which led him in mental circles until he gave up.

She'd known his name, he'd noticed, but hadn't thought to ask how. He felt drawn to her, yet something told him to be careful. It wasn't because she was foreign either. Not really foreign, but a different race. And he wasn't racist. His dad taught him to judge a man by his actions, not his words and not the colour of his skin or the way he talked. His dad also hadn't been one of those Scots who hated the English on principle. James Munro said not many people could stand up to the scrutiny of their ancestors, and if some English bastards bought out some Scottish lords several hundred years before, those Scots bore the blame for being for sale.

Munro wasn't sure if his dad's tolerance would have extended to twisted ears, but he couldn't see why not. He had to judge Eilidh by her actions, not her appearance, even if he wasn't quite sure he could wrap his head around the idea of faeries being real. But judging Eilidh by her actions meant, first and foremost, finding out what those actions had been. He'd avoided the thought because he didn't *want* her to have been involved in Robert Dewer's murder. But she knew more than she'd told him, and it was time to find out.

Technically, he shouldn't go anywhere near her. She was a witness, and he wasn't on the job until the OHA said so. But it seemed like nobody had paid much attention to Munro's report about the witness who said she'd seen an "angel". He needed to clear this up, one way or another, because something drew him to Eilidh. It wasn't necessarily sexual, although she was stunning. It felt deeper than that, like he recognised her, even though he was certain he'd never laid eyes on her before. Perhaps it was that feeling that made him believe her claims about being fae.

Munro checked his pulse and started to slow his pace. He did a fifteen-minute stretching routine, then jumped in the shower. His determination only grew, now that he'd made up his mind. He dressed and grabbed his wallet and keys, making for the door. His car was still at the police station, so he walked to the bus stop to catch the next ride into the city centre. He wouldn't have to search for her long. She was nestled in his thoughts like a pebble in his shoe. His mind pointed toward her as if she were true north.

He got off the bus in front of the city's only cinema and headed toward the High Street. She pulled him toward her. It only took two blocks to realise where he was headed—back to St Paul's, the scene of the crime.

For twenty-five years, it stood abandoned, growing more derelict with each passing season. Munro always liked the church with its octagonal base and three-story steeple, but it would never feel the same after finding the body, heartless and still. When he reached the church, Munro glanced up, past the boarded-up windows and doors. She was in there, somewhere around the third floor. He felt her stillness.

"Eilidh," he said, as softly as a whisper. A small tremor reverberated through the ancient stone. He touched a cornerstone. *Knock, knock.*

"What are you doing here?" The voice came from behind him. A copper Munro didn't know very well.

He turned and met the constable's eyes. "Just having a wee look, I suppose. Any new word?"

"I heard you were off sick or something. Too bad. CID probably would have let you in on the case, since you found the body."

His name popped into Munro's head. PC Gordon. *But what was his first name?* Munro couldn't remember. The kid was that new. "I'm all right. Be back as soon as I get word I'm cleared. Tomorrow. Maybe the next day."

Gordon eyed him suspiciously. Maybe the young PC thought he was skiving. Munro wouldn't blame him. He looked fine, and more to the point, he felt fine.

"Aye. We'll probably have it wrapped up by then."

Munro wanted to laugh. The kid didn't know what the hell he was talking about. "Oh yeah? You on the case?"

The kid straightened his uniform shirt. "I'm doing my bit." Pointedly. As though Munro wasn't doing his.

"Aye, I'll sleep better knowing that," Munro said. He glanced up at the steeple where he knew Eilidh perched. Could she hear him? He slapped his palm against the old stone wall one more time. It was warm to the touch. Alive. It stopped him in his tracks. He could feel its density and age and was suddenly aware of the shifts in the earth that had first formed it, the water that had sluiced over it, the chisel that had hewn it from its resting place. A slight glow wove through invisible faults deep in the rock.

"Hey, you all right?"

Munro removed his hand from the wall and turned to the PC. Concern had replaced suspicion on the kid's face. "I'm fine," Munro said. "Just forgot to eat this morning. I'll go grab something." He gave the kid a wave and headed off without another word. Munro didn't trust his balance, and he knew this would already come back to haunt him. He could make an excuse, but suddenly he wasn't as worried about getting back to work. Something was messing with his head. He had to talk to Eilidh.

She'd passed out too, in that very spot. She'd have to know what was going on, and he hoped she could tell him how to make it stop.

He headed toward the South Inch, relieved to feel her follow. By the time she caught up with him, he had sat on a wall near the green, just off one of the park's paths. Far enough from public view that he probably wouldn't run into anyone he knew, but close enough that she wouldn't have to hunt for him.

While he waited, Munro worked out exactly what he'd say. He'd pin her down about what she saw the night of Dewer's murder. Knowing what he did, he figured she had to be the "angel" Mrs Pentworth saw at the church. That meant Eilidh had to have seen the murder, or at least the killer. He'd get the information and then find a way to make sure Getty and Hallward got it, while at the same time leaving Eilidh out of it.

The more he considered, the more Munro realised two things. First, his gut believed her, no matter what his rational brain said. She wasn't human. Anyone who looked at her for more than five minutes would realise that. If the ears didn't give her away, those eyes would at least raise a few questions. Second, nothing good would come of exposing her to the rest of the world. At best, they'd think her some kind of illegal immigrant. Although she hadn't said so specifically, he couldn't imagine she had papers. Could a faerie even be a British citizen?

Just as he'd sorted out exactly what to say, Eilidh walked up. She slouched and covered most of her face with her hood, but he couldn't mistake her walk or her presence. She lifted her swirling eyes to meet his. As he opened his mouth to speak, she said, "What manner of magic do you have, Munro?" Her voice pierced his mind, and its haunting clarity carried an accusation.

The word *magic* struck him as funny, and the concept threw him off his stride. His planned questions fled. He went from amused to confused. "What?" He'd heard her well enough, but his brain didn't want to process her meaning.

"You cast your voice into the stone. I heard it." Again, the accusation.

"I…" Munro was suddenly bereft of words.

"You can sense the flows, yes?" Impatient now.

"I…" He wished he could say something intelligent. But in thinking about her question, some of it did make sense. If he could accept that she was different, could he accept he might be too? He'd felt a flow between them. He hadn't seen it with his eyes, but when he touched the cornerstone, something happened. Munro was so caught up in the memory that he hadn't noticed how close Eilidh had come or how intently she stared into his eyes.

"You do not have faerie blood," she said, but a question lurked in the back of her voice.

That made him laugh. "No," he said. "I'm one hundred per cent human."

Finally, she took a half-step back. "I've heard stories of humans who used to aid our people. Their magic was different, but it is said they could wield the Ways of Earth. Is stone your primary element then?"

She was speaking English, but none of her words made sense. He wanted to deny it, but some strange things had happened during the past few days.

When he didn't answer, she looked around at the ground and bent to pick a stone from the path. "Does it speak to you?" She pressed it into his hand. The stone grew warm and amplified the pull he felt from her presence. When she withdrew her hand, he locked his gaze on hers. The silver swirls in her eyes danced. She must have felt it.

He closed his hand around the stone, but it had gone quiet. He rubbed it with his fingers, but it did not seem alive as the stone at St Paul's.

"Eilidh." He stopped and swallowed. Her name filled his head, and he had to focus to keep talking. "Tell me about the night Robert Dewer was killed."

"The man below the church?"

Munro resisted asking her how many dead men he could possibly mean. He nodded and waited. Part of being a cop was knowing when to shut up and let people talk.

"Do you know, then, who killed him?" she asked.

Something in her tone set off alarms in his head. "Are you saying you do?"

She nodded. "Of course."

Munro licked his lips. He'd figured she'd seen *something* but hadn't really expected her to know the killer's name. He held perfectly still, not wanting to do anything to distract or discourage her, but inside his mind raced. He couldn't keep her name out of things if she'd seen the crime or knew the killer. He'd have to tell Hallward. He had no clue how he'd manage that, but first things first.

Eilidh sat for a long time without speaking.

Munro waited. Finally, he said, "Eilidh?"

She didn't meet his eyes. Her expression had grown distant, and she stared vaguely into the trees. "You must leave this to me, Munro. You cannot stop one who casts blood shadows."

"Eilidh," he said, more sternly this time.

She looked up. "I do not think even I can stop him. He must be an outcast like me, but I do not know his name or what kingdom exiled him. He is not of my own people, I believe." Then she went on, as though speaking to herself. "The conclave will not help, and you humans are not equipped." Again she looked at him, her tone sad. "This blood faerie will kill again, Munro. I must find him first."

A faerie did this? Munro's heart sank. He could definitely *not* take this to Hallward. The sergeant would have him on permanent disability leave so fast Munro would never know what hit him. It was all a bit much to take in, but Munro couldn't let her slip away. He didn't want her story to be the truth, but he believed her. He didn't know what kingdom or conclave she was talking about, but he could tell the news was bad. "I'll help you, Eilidh. We humans might surprise you."

He thought she might laugh, but instead she just gave a sharp nod. "You have surprised me very much, Munro. That is true."

Munro glanced down at his hands. He continued worrying the small stone in his fingers while they talked. The plain grey stone had been shaped into a smooth, arched teardrop with a curling claw at the top. He hadn't even felt himself doing it. The shape was simple, yet an elegant curve. Without knowing why, he put the stone into Eilidh's hand.

She looked intently into his eyes. "You surprise me very much indeed, Munro."

"Quinton," he said.

Confusion clouded her face. "I do not know that word."

He grinned, even though he felt the weight of the world. "It's my first name. Munro is my family name. You can call me Quinton." He wasn't sure what possessed him to do it. It wasn't exactly professional. He was a cop and she was a witness. A psycho faerie was killing humans. Yet here he stood, chatting her up in the park.

"Quinton," she repeated. It sounded rich, as her strange accent pulled a harmony of sounds from the word. "It is a name we will share between us then."

Munro didn't know what that meant, but Eilidh seemed more relaxed than she had since she arrived. Whatever bond of friendship they were forming, he had to get back to the important matter at hand. "Tell me about the murderer, Eilidh. I know you want to stop him. I do too. I can help." If he'd said those words a week ago, it would have sounded patronizing. After all, he was the cop. She was just a witness. But seeing what he'd seen in the past few days, well, maybe she knew more about this than he did. At the very least, he needed her. Without her, they'd probably never find the guy—until he killed again. Munro didn't want that to happen. He'd seen Robert Dewer's face and the gaping bloody hole in his chest, and he never wanted to see anything like it again.

Eilidh hesitated. He sensed her discomfort. Was it because of him specifically or simply because of his race? He waited patiently. It didn't seem like she was about to bolt, so the least he could do was give her a minute. Despite the sense of urgency, he found the silence between them comfortable.

Finally, she said, "I have decided to tell you of this blood faerie, Quinton. If I am going to be Watcher for this city, I will need help. It is not easy, you understand, to ask for the help of a human, but you are something more." She paused. "And I like you. You know how to be silent."

Munro started to smile, but his smile faded as Eilidh told him what she knew of the murder.

CHAPTER 8

CRIDHE SAT IN THE DARKNESS of the craggy cave, staring at the twin hearts in the recess above. They beat in the slow time that human hearts did, and their matched pace made his faerie blood calm to meet their rhythm.

Robert Dewer's heart had veins of icy blue, indicating his impressive talents in winter magic. Cridhe had kept the small, wooden whistle Robert used to call the wind. He had not been close to Robert. But now, seeing Robert's heart as it beat on the cold stone shelf, Cridhe said a prayer to the Father of the Azure to honour the sacrifice. Cridhe did not usually care for such things, but Dudlach would have insisted on the show of respect.

The other heart, Jon Anderson's, had the golden glow of rare fire magic coursing through it, pulsing in each chamber, imprisoned in the fleshy organ. Cridhe had kept nothing of Jon's, but he hadn't been the one to harvest Jon's heart.

Dudlach said they needed one of each of the four elements of earth to feed the source stone and finish the ritual. It had to be Jon first then. Among their faithful were already plenty of air and water druids. But another fire? No, unlikely. And best to do it before it became too *difficult*, Dudlach said with that knowing look.

Cridhe knew the real reason was that Dudlach hadn't liked Cridhe and Jon becoming...friends. Jon had understood Cridhe's needs at all levels. But Cridhe hadn't been able to refuse Dudlach's demand. To confess an attachment demonstrated weakness.

So Jon had to die. Cridhe stared at the heart, disturbed that he couldn't feel Jon's presence. He'd hoped that in preserving Jon's magic, he would preserve some of his soul. It hadn't worked, but still Cridhe sat and watched the beating heart. It dismayed him that Dudlach, the one whose voice he least wanted to hear, was the ghost who'd attached itself to him.

Cridhe told the humans, the other faithful, that Jon betrayed them. He'd shown them his still beating heart and secured their loyalty. If Cridhe could kill him, the obvious favourite among the group, they all had reason to fear. Cridhe hated the lie, but he could not deny it had done wonders. They had seen the faerie's magic, but this was so much more. Some were sickened and afraid, but two had shown a promising ruthless hunger when they'd seen Jon's sacrifice. It was those two Cridhe went to speak with now.

Cridhe had warded the cave so humans would have an aversion to entering it or even wanting to think too much about it, so he made his way to a nearby clearing where Aaron and Jay waited. They stood and bowed their heads when he approached. They were flawlessly subservient, and Cridhe enjoyed it. Not in the same way Jon had been, but he doubted he would again find someone so perfectly suited to him. Jon's fire magic had flowed so effortlessly with Cridhe's blood shadows. It created something—

"Master?" Jay said, keeping his eyes lowered.

Cridhe scowled at the interruption to his reverie. Stupid humans were always in such a hurry. He raised a haughty eyebrow.

"You seem angry. Have we done something wrong?"

Cridhe waved his hand, dismissing the thought. "Today you will find Craig Laughlin. Make sure he drinks no spirits and eats no meat."

Jay and Aaron exchanged a glance. "But—" Aaron began.

Jay cut him off, keeping his eyes on Cridhe and displaying the right amount of fear. "Yes, Master," he said, giving Aaron a firm shake of his head. "Where should we meet you?"

Cridhe smiled. At least one of them seemed to understand. He considered the question. It didn't matter where, as long as it was outside the sphere of kingdom influence, so it had to be an area populated by humans. He liked the idea of going back to Perth, to lay this third sacrifice at Eilidh's feet, so to speak. He wanted to impress her, but he couldn't let himself get too close again. Not until he was sure she was ready for him.

"Where do you live, Aaron?"

"Over at Muirton," the man said, his face plainly showing he didn't like the direction Cridhe was taking.

"Isn't there a school nearby?"

"The Grammar is just down the way. Off Gowans."

Cridhe nodded. "That's the one. Bring him there. I'll meet you two hours past dark." He did not intend to pay any mind to human timekeeping. He would come when he was ready, and they would wait. He knew that, and so did they.

∞

Breaking about the hundredth rule that day, Munro opened his front door and stood aside so Eilidh could enter. By this time, he figured he was in so deep that one more thing wasn't going to tip the scales. When darkness started to fall in the park, he'd felt hungry, tired, and exposed. The only problem was that Eilidh had insisted they walk to his house rather than taking the bus or catching a cab. He watched her as they walked together and saw how warily she kept an eye on the cars. She seemed more concerned about them than any of the people they passed.

He also noticed that she tended to watch and assess like a cop. She would take it all in, categorise, weigh, and filter, as though constantly calculating threats. When she told him about the murder, she'd also had to explain quite a bit about herself and her past. He knew she'd been the faerie equivalent of a cop or maybe military was closer to the mark. She called herself a Watcher, and he thought that was a pretty good description of what he did as well.

What he didn't understand was her exile. She glossed over it and said it didn't concern him. Now wasn't the time to press, but he wanted answers. He didn't know what kind of crime a faerie could commit that would merit exile, but from the solemn frown on her face, he knew she hadn't been caught crossing against a red light.

He stood for a long moment, holding the front door open. Eilidh peered into the darkened entryway from the front step. She glanced up and down the street, obviously uncomfortable ever since they'd entered his neighbourhood. She didn't seem to like the feel of the houses. Finally, she met his eyes. "You enter first, Quinton."

He loved the way she said his name like a secret. Slipping his keys into his pocket, he stepped inside and flicked on the lights. When she didn't come in right away, he said, "In your own time." He left the front door open and went to see if he had anything in the kitchen to offer a guest. He never really had company. He'd dated some in recent years, but rarely, if ever, brought anyone home.

When he turned, Eilidh had come in, hugging her arms as though certain the place might collapse around her. Considering that he'd found her in a crumbling old church, he didn't understand her fear. "Everything okay?" He'd never seen her so vulnerable.

She nodded and then suddenly seemed flustered. "I have no hearth gift to offer."

He tilted his head and smiled at her, hoping to put her at ease. She wasn't human. Every little comment or look gave him more evidence, and his belief became more solid, even though he didn't know what to make of it. "A gift is not traditional for us. Would you like a drink? I have beer, orange juice, or I can put the kettle on."

"Put it on what?"

Munro stifled a grin. "I mean I can make tea or coffee, if you prefer."

Her gaze continued to roam around his house, taking in the kitchen, with special note of the appliances. She glanced toward the living area. Her unease made him want to comfort her.

"Would you like me to show you around first?"

She nodded and followed him into the living room. He took her from room to room. She touched everything, noticing the thin layer of dust around the place. When they were in his exercise room, she asked him about the treadmill. "What does this machine do?"

"You've really never been inside a house before?"

Eilidh shook her head. "I've seen things through windows, but it is different being inside, touching it. There is much I've never understood and had no one to ask."

He nodded, wondering what it would be like to be so completely alone in the world. Gesturing to the treadmill he said, "It's for exercise. Want to see?" Munro pushed a button on the front panel and stepped onto it, keeping it at the lowest, and therefore quietest, setting. He began to walk, holding the bars at the side.

Eilidh grinned. "It lets you walk and go nowhere?"

"I usually run," he said, "But, yes."

She started to laugh. The sound was earthy and rich. It made him aware of how much he wanted her. The intensity of his reaction caught him by surprise.

Munro turned off the treadmill and stepped down. Suddenly afraid of what would happen if he stood still, he continued the tour. Along the way, she investigated all the closets, asked him about the water heater and radiators, and wanted to see how to turn the lamps on and off. She remarked how many more devices people owned than they used to and how she observed the way people's pockets buzzed and jingled and beeped constantly these days.

When they came to his bedroom, she walked right in, not seeming to notice he hesitated at the doorway. She smiled as though she discovered something important. "You have no machines in here, Quinton."

He hadn't really thought about it before, but he didn't like to watch TV in bed, and he used the alarm on his smartphone. He hated the glow of digital alarm clocks. His bedroom, like the rest of his house, was furnished simply. He had a bed, a dresser covered in framed family pictures, a wide, comfortable chair, and a bookcase.

Eilidh went to the bookcase and ran her fingers over the spines. "You are a scholar?"

He couldn't help but laugh. "No, those are mostly fiction." You wouldn't think a cop would like to read about fictional detectives, but he did. Peter James, Ian Rankin, even some old Conan Doyle and Agatha Christie. It did drive him a little crazy how easy they made it all seem, like the toughest of cases could be wrapped up in a few days or that the countryside was crawling with serial killers, but he found them an enjoyable read. He also liked biographies and books about history, particularly of Scotland.

Munro found himself wondering if Eilidh could read, but he thought it would be impolite to ask. She could speak English well enough, although it was obviously not her first language. But she certainly hadn't gone to the local high school. He had trouble imagining a forest full of faerie kids learning their ABCs. Did faeries have schools of some sort? Just when he'd decided to ask, she opened the door to the master bathroom and flicked on the light.

"You have two other rooms like this, but smaller."

"Yeah, this place has three loos, although the first one is just a toilet and sink. We call the smallest one a *cloakroom*."

Eilidh looked him up and down as though noting his lack of a cloak, but she made no comment. Instead, she stepped forward and peered into the toilet. "This is for drinking? It's very low."

"Uh, no. It's for…" He was completely at a loss. What could he say? She watched him closely, and he could feel her analysing his discomfort. It hadn't occurred to him until just then that she'd likely never seen a toilet. If she hadn't been inside a home and avoided public places, she wouldn't have had an opportunity. The church she lived in didn't have any fixtures left. It was an empty husk of a building. He couldn't help but wonder what facilities she used. That thought only made the conversation more awkward.

"For what?"

"Shitting," he finally said. It wasn't what he wanted to say, but he also didn't want to find her drinking out of a toilet because he'd been too embarrassed to explain things.

She didn't appear offended. Instead, she nodded and went to the sink. "For washing?"

Munro stepped next to her and turned one of the faucets. "Right side for cold water. Left side for hot water. See? The red dot on the top means hot. But sometimes it takes a few seconds for the water to warm up, so you have to be careful."

She turned both faucets on and off a couple times, then nodded. "And this is the same?" she asked, gesturing to the shower.

He turned the taps and pulled the stopper to divert the tub water to the showerhead. "The sink is for washing your hands and face. This is for washing all of you."

Eilidh's eyes lit up. "It's like rain inside your house."

Before he could say another word, she'd peeled off her sweatshirt and thin t-shirt, kicked off her shoes, and wiggled out of her jeans. The first thing he noticed was that she didn't wear any underwear, top nor bottom. The second thing he noticed was the beautiful pale sheen of her skin. It was like smooth, pinkish pearls and nearly hairless. Her nipples were like delicate cherries on her small round breasts.

He caught his breath and realised he was staring. With a jerk, he turned away and stepped out of the bathroom. "I'll get you a towel." He stepped into the hallway where he kept linens and found a large, fluffy blue towel in his mismatched collection.

It took him a moment to catch his breath. What the hell was he doing? He glanced back toward the bedroom. He wanted her, no doubt about that, but did she want him? She was almost childlike with her innocent curiosity, but she was anything *but* a child. He hadn't worked out the math, but he guessed she was much older than he was, no matter how young she appeared. So why did he feel like he would be taking advantage of her? She was a bundle of contradictions, both strong and smart, part of a magical world he'd never imagined, and yet she seemed vulnerable. He could tell she was afraid. Maybe not of him, specifically, but of the human world.

By the time he returned to the bathroom, she had turned off the water and stepped onto the tile floor. He tried to hand her the towel without completely entering and avoided staring at her creamy skin. He kept his eyes on her feet and the huge puddle that was spreading around her.

"What is wrong, Quinton? You have gone red. Did I use the washing compartment incorrectly?"

"Uh, no," he said. *God help me. I'm blushing?*

She took the towel. "What is this for?"

"To dry yourself."

She muttered a few words, and tingling spread over his skin. He couldn't help but stare at her now. Air rushed around the room strongly enough to knock over a mostly-empty bottle of mouthwash near the hand basin. "I'm not strong in the Ways of Earth, but I can at least dry myself." She tutted as though he'd said something slightly condescending, but her smile was genuine. She seemed completely relaxed and at home as she handed the towel back.

The way she looked at him propelled him forward. He saw an invitation in her eyes, so when he took the towel, he stepped closer and put his arms around her, touching the impossibly soft skin of her back. She tensed, but didn't resist when he put his lips tenderly on hers. The kiss was gentle and tentative. As he tasted her, he wanted her even more and it grew deeper.

After a moment, she put her hands to his chest and pushed him away. "Quinton," she said in a firm, scolding tone. "You must not do that. I am fae and you are human." She bent to pick up her discarded clothing, and he averted his eyes. She walked past him into the bedroom and pulled on her jeans as though nothing had happened. She straightened and turned a curious expression on him. "You do understand, don't you?"

When he saw pity in her eyes, it hit him like a sucker punch. He'd never felt so embarrassed in his life. "Oh god," he said. "You feel fine walking around naked in front of me just like I wouldn't think twice about undressing in front of a dog." He'd fancied girls before that didn't return the feelings, but he'd never felt as rejected and bereft as he did right then. If he'd been anywhere but in his own house, he'd have walked out the front door without another word. He wanted her, more desperately than he'd wanted anyone, and she had as much attraction to him as she might the family pet.

A cloud passed over Eilidh's face, and she covered her small breasts with her hands, as though aware of her nudity for the first time. "I've done something wrong."

He started to leave to let her finish dressing. He couldn't stand talking to her when she stood there topless with her jeans unbuttoned. Her delicate fingers reached out and closed over his bicep. "Quinton," she said, with the same intensity that had melted him before. "I am not good with humans. I have lived among you for decades, but I have never had a friend among you. I do not fully understand your ways."

Munro did his best to give her a convincing smile. "It's fine, Eilidh. Really."

She searched his eyes with those swirling pools of silver. "You're lying to me."

"Yeah," he said. "I am." He squeezed her hand and removed her fingers from his arm. He felt like a jerk. He was horny, she didn't want him, and now he was being an arsehole about it. "I'll be okay, Eilidh. I just need a minute."

He left her in his bedroom and went to the kitchen to get a beer. *I am such a moron.* He tried to think of a way to make things right and erase the awkwardness. His idiotic libido couldn't be allowed to get in the way of the case. How could he have let himself forget why he was talking to her in the first place? As soon as she came out, he'd make sure they talked about the case and only that. He'd keep his mind out of her pants and focus on catching the blood faerie before he killed again.

When half an hour passed and she didn't appear, Munro returned to the bedroom. He had to apologise; he knew that. He'd been an idiot—and insensitive. Of course she wouldn't be attracted to him. It was probably her magical nature that made him feel this unbearable pull. He imagined all humans might react that way to the fae. It made perfect sense and probably explained why she'd kept to herself. Considering that she'd been exiled and forced to live in the city, he felt even more of a tool.

When he opened the bedroom door, he turned immediately to the open window. Eilidh had gone. Sitting on his dresser was the stone teardrop he'd given her at the park.

CHAPTER 9

SAOR STEPPED OUT of the shadows, startling her.

"Well, that was—"

"Shut up," Eilidh said. She walked around him, wanting to put some distance between herself and the rows of box-like human houses. She didn't even bother to ask why Saor had spied on her. He'd obviously seen everything, judging by his haughtier-than-usual expression.

Saor easily caught up with her and kept stride. "You have needs, I suppose, and little hope of meeting one of our kind in the foreseeable future."

She felt venom in his voice, as though he'd caught her doing something shameful. She supposed he had, but she couldn't see that it was any of his business—not anymore. "You should dress more appropriately if you're going to come into the city, Saor."

He waved a dismissive hand as they crossed a major street and he continued to follow her west. "I have remained unseen."

They were already in the northwest part of the city, so she made for Huntingtower, an old estate with large grounds surrounded by farmland. The nearest building other than the ancient Huntingtower Castle was a nearby country hotel. It was close enough to the human populations that the kingdom influence was almost imperceptible, even at the darkest summer hour. Eilidh didn't like to risk being outside the highway that ringed the city, and this was as far as she would usually dare go. Tonight, though, she felt strange. Angry, but not the vague anger at the injustice of her exile. That anger would normally be tempered by her own sense of guilt about her malformed magic. She didn't even know who she was angry at. Munro, perhaps, for kissing her, at herself for letting it happen, for forgetting where she was, at Saor for having the indecency to witness the whole humiliating incident.

Eilidh stepped recklessly in front of a car on the A9, causing it to swerve. Saor grabbed her arm and whisked her across the road. Soon they made it to the nearby farmland, and Saor spun her around and put his hands on her shoulders. "By Faith, what is wrong with you?"

His anger only excited hers. "You know truly what is wrong with me. Or didn't the conclave explain it to you? I seem to remember a decree was issued on the matter."

"Do you care for him?" Saor's face was still in the moonlight. His perfect lack of expression spoke volumes to Eilidh. She could feel his tension.

"Of course not. He's human, for the love of the Mother."

"He appears to care for you."

Eilidh shook his hands away and sat in the middle of the fragrant green field. "Don't be ridiculous. That wasn't caring you saw through the windows, but friendship. I think humans associate nudity with sexuality. He believed I was requesting a sexual encounter. As a friend, he did what he thought I wanted him to do." She sighed. "They appear enough like us that, after a time, it's easy to forget their ways are so different." Eilidh reflected that she'd never forgotten before, and Saor did not challenge her.

Saor sat beside her as Eilidh stewed. She had confused Munro, and she didn't know enough about him to make things right. It had been cowardly to leave, but she couldn't bear having to confess her ignorance. It was bad enough that she'd had to tell him about her exile. He'd wanted to know about her...disability...her crimes, but she was too ashamed to tell him. One chance, she'd had. One chance in twenty-five years for a friendship, some connection beyond watching from her tower and talking only with rats and spiders, and she'd ruined it with her ignorance and fear.

Her anger resurfaced, and she aimed it squarely at Saor. "What are you doing here, anyway, spying like a naughty child or scorned lover?" She glanced to the stars, checking the time. "Shouldn't you be on watch?"

"Apparently I've been reduced to messenger boy."

She started to lash out at his spiteful tone, but stopped herself when she realised what he'd said. "You have a message? From the conclave?" Her heart thumped with excitement. "Are they sending help?"

Suddenly, Saor's anger left, replaced by a twist of compassion. "No, Eilidh. You should not hope they will have a change of heart."

She swallowed her disappointment and nodded. "Who then?"

"Imire."

"My father? What message did he send?"

"He wishes to see you, if you will risk it."

Ah, then he would not come to her. It was rare for any faerie to leave the kingdom. They had an innate attraction to the Halls of Mist and the Otherworld. To travel where they could no longer feel it, well, none would do it by choice. Even Saor would not be here if he had not felt compelled by loyalty to Imire. Eilidh wanted to believe she'd grown accustomed to the loss, but it still haunted her, even more so now, since she'd been in kingdom lands so recently and felt the longing return. "Where?"

"He said he would come to the folly."

She nodded. It was a good choice. Atop a hill overlooking the city, a Scottish lord had built a tower over two hundred years ago. It was difficult to reach and rested on the edge of kingdom influence during the night, when no human would attempt the steep hiking trails. A footpath led to the stone structure, perched atop a three-hundred-foot sheer drop. The heights were home mostly to peregrines. "When?"

"Tomorrow night when the bear ascends to the weaver's peak."

Eilidh nodded. She too still kept time by the stars, even though no one else in the city did. She supposed she should learn to follow the human clocks. The numbers on the dial did not confuse her as much as the talk. *Half-past* and *quarter-to* they would say, *tea time* or *noon*. She wondered if Munro might teach her. Her thoughts returned to the kiss. It would have been wrong to take advantage of him, wrong to use a human in such a way. But it had been a very long time since anyone touched her out of desire, much less kissed her. The last, of course, had been Saor, decades ago. He had been the most handsome faerie she'd ever seen. She loved his unusual golden hair and his sense of humour. They used to laugh together. Everything between them had been easy and fun. She stole a glance at him in the darkness and found he was watching her intently.

"I used to be able to read your mind," he said. "Now your thoughts are closed to me." The Ways of Earth did not actually enable the fae to read minds, but he had known her so well back then, he could read every mood.

"Seeing you these past days has brought back memories."

"Not unpleasant ones, I hope."

She smiled. "No, not unpleasant ones." She tried to put the thoughts behind her. Time had eased the sharpness of the longing for her old life.

"I will meet you at the folly then," Saor said and stood to go.

It pained Eilidh, reminding her that she should not grow accustomed to even these brief visits. "Will you?"

"Imire asked me to stand guard."

It alarmed Eilidh that her father thought they would need protection. Was he still watched because of her escape? She always thought if she were careful and stayed away from even the fringes of the kingdom territory, she would be safe. She hoped none would care enough about her life or death to make an effort to find her. But if Imire wanted a guard, he either feared for Eilidh or for himself. She stood and turned to Saor, searching his face.

"Don't worry, Eilidh. I won't let anyone hurt you."

Eilidh could not deny that his words comforted her.

∞

After Eilidh left, Munro took a shower, trying hard to ignore the memory of her standing naked in that small space. He felt tired and overwhelmed and paced about the house like a caged animal. He went to the fridge and reached in. He'd just cracked open his second beer when he felt a sudden alarm. He turned east. A sense of dread made his hands shake. The open can fell to the linoleum. A scream filled his head. Then as quickly as it had come, it ceased, leaving a horrible, empty silence. Munro felt a loss, but he could not place it. Without a doubt, something *wrong* had happened.

It felt like his hunches sometimes did, but with a clarity he'd never experienced. So either what had just happened was worse than anything he'd ever encountered, including the murder of Robert Dewer, or something in him had changed more than he realised. He knew, however, it was a murder.

Munro's first instinct was to call Getty and ask him to pick him up right away. His car was still at the police station, and a taxi would take too long. But as he strode toward the phone in the hall, he realised it wouldn't be the best move. Sure, Getty and even Sergeant Hallward knew about Munro's hunches, but there was no way he could explain being the first on the scene for two murders, especially if the second hadn't been called in yet. That would move him to the top of the CID suspect list, if they even had one.

Munro got a towel, mopped up the beer, and thought hard. His adrenaline had kicked in, making him too jittery to do the smart thing, which was to wait. Tossing the towel into the sink, he started to pace. He asked himself what Getty would do, but dismissed it as soon as he thought it. Getty would turn on the telly and wait it out. His partner didn't believe in hunches, except maybe Munro's. Even then, Munro could tell Getty didn't like them much.

Hallward would tell Munro to take his meds, go to bed, and see the doc first thing.

Munro asked himself what Eilidh would do. She, more than anyone, understood the danger and what was at stake. She certainly wouldn't sit around waiting for someone else to call. Not that they would. Munro was supposed to be on sick leave. He wasn't even a major part of the case, so who would think to keep him posted?

Munro went to the hallway and pulled the telephone plug out of the wall, strode out the front door, and locked it behind him. He wished he had his car, but he didn't need it. Whatever happened had been close. The after-effects of the violence hung in the air like debris after a bomb detonation.

He walked through his neighbourhood's curving streets until he reached the easiest access to a main road. Between the railway that cut through a steep gully nearby and the odd triangle of twisted roads, it took him longer to get out than he would have liked. The advantage of living in a neighbourhood that was tucked away turned into a disadvantage of tangled streets and frustration. His instincts led one way, but the confusion of good-intentioned civil engineering took him another.

At least there was little traffic along Dunkeld Road this time of night, and crossing on foot didn't prove much of a problem. Even though his feeling of dread intensified, Munro's steps grew faster as he ducked into the Muirton housing estate. The darkness drew him past the rows of terraced houses and flats as he turned along Bute Road, keeping to the shadows on the left as much as he could. At this time of night, no one loitered around the bus stops. He was close now. He felt it. As soon as the fences surrounding the Perth Grammar School came into view, he knew he'd find the body there.

The extra time it took to walk around the school pained him, but he didn't want to be seen, just in case someone had already called the police. Or worse yet, if they hadn't. Within a few minutes, he was in the back garden of property that backed onto the school's. He jumped the fence with little effort and went into an overgrown grassy field.

That's when he heard the strange clicking noise. He couldn't see much in the darkness. "Quinton. This way," Eilidh said.

Munro picked his way through the uneven scrubby ground to where she was hunkered down. He squatted beside her, following her gaze toward the high school. "Another murder?"

She turned to him in the darkness, her silver-green eyes glowing brightly. "You felt it?"

"A little while ago. Took me a few to get here though. Has anyone called it in?"

"Your police? I don't know."

They both stared toward the scene of the crime. Munro felt the dark wrongness hanging in the air.

"Come," Eilidh said. "The blood faerie went south."

They backtracked away from the body, and Munro felt a stab of guilt. He should make sure the crime had been reported. His training told him he should preserve the scene and stay with the body. If he left, who knew what would happen? And who would discover the corpse? This was a school, he reminded himself. He didn't want some kid stumbling upon the horror. But he also knew Eilidh was right, and, for Munro, doing the *right* thing, the thing his years of training told him to do, would be a mistake. It would lead to questions Munro didn't have answers to, and would confuse an investigation doomed to fail anyway, at least as long as the police were searching for a human culprit with ordinary motives. Preserving forensic evidence wouldn't tell them half as much as using Eilidh to track the killer.

Munro couldn't sense the presence or scent Eilidh followed through town. He could tell she was frustrated at having to jog slowly enough to accommodate his human limitations, but she didn't leave him behind. She covered her features with a hood as they moved into the more trafficked streets. Fortunately, the one they chased seemed to have avoided well-lit areas and took back streets wherever possible.

After about a mile of dense city, they moved more openly and picked up their pace. Eilidh stopped from time to time and stood perfectly still, listening hard. Then she would shake her head, and they'd go on, rarely deviating from a path that led straight south. After another mile, they passed the large expanse of the South Inch, down the Edinburgh Road to the edge of the city.

Eilidh stopped again, gazing south, and quivering. "He was just here." Frustration rippled across her face. "Faith, I can go no further."

Heart thumping from the long run across the city, Munro stared at her, confused. "Did the trail disappear?"

"No," she said. "It is too dangerous. There are other fae about. Kingdom fae. I can feel the borders of the Otherworld nearby."

"Eilidh, I don't understand. Are you saying this murderer is a kingdom faerie? I thought they were the good guys."

She snorted. "Good? You would think..." She locked her eyes on Munro's, and he felt the intensity of her stare. "How is it that he is able to walk the borderlands freely when I cannot?" She paced back and forth on an invisible border, staring south.

Munro followed her line of sight. "What do you mean?" He knew an immense quarry was hidden from view just beyond those trees. Then came the highway, and then nothing but farms and woodland for quite a distance. There would be the odd village tucked along a B-road, but not a lot of civilisation.

"He must be an outcast, like me. None who know the Path of the Azure would be welcome within the kingdom. And yet he is not afraid to continue on."

"He's a psychopath."

"I do not know this word," she said, flicking her hood back with impatience.

"He must be crazy to do the things he's done. He's not going to think like you or I would."

"Crazy?" She stared at him.

"Isn't he? How could a sane person commit these murders?"

"There is a difference between evil and insane."

Munro didn't understand why Eilidh seemed so annoyed with him all of a sudden. "So he's not afraid of the kingdom fae. What does it matter?"

"It matters," she said.

Eilidh suddenly whipped her head around as though she'd heard something. Her eyes widened with shock, and she crouched, ready to leap. "Where are you?" she shouted into the darkness.

"What is it?" Munro asked. "What's happening?"

"Run!" she cried out. "Go away from here."

"I'm not leaving until you tell me what's going on."

She spun. "No!" she shouted, turning to Munro, her face going alabaster white. She looked like she was about to speak, but then she collapsed.

Munro kept alert and watched the trees as he knelt and touched Eilidh's neck. Her pulse was strong, faster than he would have expected, but she was alive. Standing and turning slowly, Munro listened. He couldn't hear a sound from the trees, not so much as the peep of a mouse or a rustle of wind.

He glanced down and saw Eilidh move. She groaned and her eyelids fluttered, but she did not speak.

"Come on," he said. "Let's get you out of here."

Cursing that he had no phone and no car, he slipped his arm underneath hers. A few blocks to the north, he would find a pub with a telephone. He could call a taxi from there.

Although she had a slight build, Eilidh was solid and heavier than she first appeared. Rather than throw her over his shoulder, he tried to carry her as though propping up a drunken friend. People would accept the latter without question, but a burly guy carrying a woman fireman-style? That might draw second looks. When a taxi finally picked them up, the driver seemed concerned that he'd have to clean up after a couple of drunks. Munro stuck a twenty in the driver's hand up front, so at least he wouldn't worry about them skipping out on the fare.

The night was nearly gone by the time they made it into Munro's house. Eilidh still had not regained consciousness. She groaned and muttered, but seemed stuck in a nightmare from which she couldn't wake.

He carried her inside and laid her on his bed, removing her strange leather shoes. He took off his own shoes and shirt and stretched his aching back. It had been a long, tiresome night. He worried about Eilidh, about the case, and about the undiscovered body over at the Grammar.

Exhaustion overtook him. He thought about bunking on the sofa, but wanted to be close in case Eilidh woke up. The last thing he needed was to discover she'd climbed out the window again. He still didn't know why she'd done that, and they hadn't spoken of it. When they saw each other at the school, the awkwardness disappeared in the face of other important matters. Now that they were alone and the urgency had passed, he feared the strained feeling would return the second she woke up.

He watched her in the moonlight, her small mouth slightly open and her long white lashes fluttering. He wished he could reach into her nightmare and make it stop. All he could do was hold her hand and whisper goodnight, hoping she would wake in the morning.

CHAPTER 10

A LOUD RINGING CAUSED Eilidh to wake with a start. It took her a moment to recognise Munro's bedroom. She lay on his bed, fully dressed and alone, although the rumpled linens told her he must have lain next to her.

She heard voices down the hall. Slipping on her shoes, she stepped into the corridor and crept closer to the source of the sounds. She saw Munro's visitor through the glass-paned interior door that led into the living room, but unfortunately, it kept her from catching every word, even with her excellent hearing.

A man wearing a police uniform sat in one of the large padded seats humans seemed to prefer in their homes. Eilidh could detect the scent of fried food, sweat, and cigarettes lingering near the entryway. The visitor's voice was low, nearly a whisper, and he seemed serious and tense. Eilidh could not see Munro's face, because he sat with his back to her, but she noticed how they leaned forward when they talked.

They spoke about the previous night's death, and it frustrated her that she couldn't make out more. She didn't know how humans could stand to live in these box-houses, where they couldn't feel the sun and rain or hear the wind.

Just as she was calculating whether she would be able to hear better from the kitchen, Munro's guest stood. When he did, their eyes met. Eilidh panicked and took a step back. How could she be so stupid and slow as to let someone see her here? But if she ran, would that look worse?

The guest gestured toward her and said something to Munro, who stood. She didn't know what to do, so she waited.

Munro gave her an encouraging smile and beckoned her closer. He opened the door and stepped toward her. Leaning close, he whispered, "Cover your ears."

In a well-practiced movement, Eilidh pulled up the hood of her light jacket. If the other man thought it odd, he didn't say anything, although he did seem surprised to find he wasn't the only guest in Munro's house.

"This is my friend Eilidh," Munro said to the other man. "Eilidh, this is my partner, Andrew Getty."

Getty kept glancing back and forth between Eilidh and Munro, a smile creeping over his face. He extended his hand to Eilidh. "Haley," he said. "Nice to meet you."

Munro corrected him. "Ay-lee, without an H."

Eilidh hesitated, unsure what to do with his outstretched hand. She awkwardly slipped her hand into his for a moment, and felt his strength as he squeezed her fingers and gave her hand a firm downward shake.

"Sorry," Getty said. "Eilidh. Pretty name. Is it French?"

Eilidh couldn't help but smile. "No," she said.

After a slight pause, Getty looked at Eilidh then back at Munro with a knowing grin. "I thought you were supposed to be off sick."

Munro laughed. "Believe me, I'll be back as soon as they'll let me. I went to see the doctor this morning. He didn't like it, but I got him to approve me going back tomorrow. He said I needed more rest because he didn't like the unexplained seizure, but the labs didn't show anything, so I was able to convince him to sign off."

"As long as you aren't enjoying yourself *too* much," Getty said.

"You went out this morning?" Eilidh asked and glanced toward the window. It was too overcast for her to tell the time.

"I let you sleep," he said.

Then Eilidh realised what Getty had been getting at. "Quinton," she said. "You did not tell me you had a seizure." She turned to look into his eyes.

He took her hand and enveloped it in his own. "I'm fine. Promise. It's just something I had to take care of so I can go back to work." He kissed her cheek.

She nodded, but didn't believe that was the end of the story. She had seen how disoriented he was when she first saw him in the woods. But she didn't press him, because she wasn't sure how much he would want Getty to know. The kiss surprised her as well, but perhaps that too was for Getty's benefit. From the grins he was giving Munro, Getty obviously thought Eilidh was his lover. For whatever reason, Munro allowed him to nurture the belief. Uncertain of the dynamic between the two men, she decided to let it go. Munro would have his reasons.

Munro thanked Getty for dropping by, an expression Eilidh found both curious and amusing, and for returning his phone and car. As soon as the other man was out the door, Munro let go of Eilidh's hand. "Sorry about that," he said. "How are you feeling?" A frown creased his tanned forehead. "You had me worried last night. I wouldn't have left you this morning if I hadn't had to go to see the doctor. If I'd missed the appointment, I'd have been dead meat."

Eilidh brushed aside his concern. "I'm fine." The last thing she wanted to talk about was what happened to her last night, hearing that voice in her head, feeling wave after wave of the blood shadows until they overwhelmed her and she lost consciousness. The blood faerie had led her into a trap, knowing she would follow. He was angry with her, and his rage and confusion frightened her. She didn't want to admit to Munro that perhaps he had been right. Perhaps this faerie *was* insane. The thought ran contrary to everything she believed about her race, but his ravings made little sense. Munro wouldn't understand either, and she needed to talk to someone who would, but she would have to wait for that. She changed the subject. "Did Andrew Getty bring word of the murder?"

Munro nodded. "A group of teenagers were cutting through the field around nine this morning. They found the body and called 999."

Every time Munro spoke, Eilidh realised how much of human culture was alien to her. She didn't understand many of the expressions he used, but at least she picked up the gist of it. She also noticed that he minded that those who found the body were teens. At that age, a faerie would be considered little more than an infant, in human terms, and wouldn't leave their parents' care. Humans aged faster, and their teenaged offspring were permitted to act nearly as freely as adults.

"So now they know a killer stalks your people." Eilidh had hoped to find a way to stop the murders before the human police became aware of that. The greater the crimes, the more police would be involved, and the harder her job would be. With their usual minimal influence and her own speed and power, she managed to avoid the police, at least before her first encounter with Munro. But if they started watching vigorously, she would have to be more careful. That would cost her time.

"Did you know this murder was different?" Munro asked.

"Different how?" Eilidh had not gotten close to the body. She'd focused on catching the blood faerie and hadn't thought much about the victim.

"The heart wasn't taken."

"No? Did he take something else?" Taking the heart of the first victim seemed to be part of a ritual, so this second killing must have served some purpose. Unless he had truly gone insane.

"No, but he tried. He succeeded in a way. The chest was opened as in the first murder, and the heart removed. The SOCOs found the heart a few yards away from the body."

"He left it behind?" Eilidh frowned.

"In pieces. The closest they could figure, it exploded or burst from the inside. They're hoping the autopsy will tell them more, but we both know that's unlikely."

Munro watched her closely. She realised he must wonder whether she knew more than she had told him. They stood, looking at each other for a long moment. Finally, Munro said, "We have to stop this guy. I can tell you're holding back from me, but I don't get why. Is it because of the kiss? I'm not going to push you. I'm a big boy. I can take it. And this case is more important than working out my feelings." He smiled when he said it, but Eilidh could see a residual hurt in his eyes.

It stunned her. She'd convinced herself that he'd only been doing what he thought she wanted. But now he was confessing that he felt something for her? "Munro," she said. "I am fae."

Annoyance flitted over his features. "You keep bloody saying that as though I'd forget it. You think I can be around you without seeing how different you are?" Munro looked away for a moment and then turned his blue eyes back to her. "I didn't mean to say all that," he said quietly. "I just want you to know you can trust me. It doesn't have to be awkward between us."

"It's not that I don't trust you," she explained. "I know you want to stop this killing as much as I do, even though we have somewhat different reasons. I do not know if we will be successful. I have never encountered someone such as the faerie who is killing with blood shadows. It would have frightened me even if I had every kingdom Watcher at my back. But instead I have to face it alone."

"That's my point. You aren't alone. I'm right here."

"You are—"

"Not fae? Yeah, I get that. I'm different, but I'm here, I'm willing, and I'm *not* afraid. I might be different, but I'm not less." His anger had risen, and she saw the intensity of his feeling shine brightly in his eyes.

"No," she agreed. "Not less." She wanted to explain the things he couldn't possibly appreciate about the dangers they faced. It could cost them their lives and that of many more humans. "It will take some time for me to become accustomed to this new way. I've avoided your people for decades. I don't think you less." She meant that too, possibly for the first time. The more she talked with Quinton, the more she questioned everything she had been taught about humans. She couldn't let go of her reservations, but for now, it felt nice not to be alone. She wondered if there was something more as she peered into his eyes.

His face softened as she spoke, and she was relieved to see the anger drain out of him. "Oh," he said. "I almost forgot. I got you something while I was out." He went to the living room and retrieved a plastic bag. When he returned, he said, "I nearly picked one with flowers, but decided it wouldn't suit you. You look good in black." He pulled something knitted out of the bag, tore off a plastic tag, and handed it to her.

"What is it?" she said, turning the object over in her hands. It was shaped like a cloth bowl.

Munro grinned. "Here." He took it and stretched the fabric, then nestled it over her head. "It's called a watch cap and will save you from messing with that silly hood all the time." He adjusted it snugly on her head, then gently reached over and made sure her ears were fully tucked in on both sides.

Eilidh shivered. He must not have known what an intimate gesture caressing ears was to her people. His face betrayed no sexual intent, but she couldn't help but respond to the touch.

"Are you cold?" he asked. "I can turn on the heat."

"No," she said, feeling the edges of the hat. The fact that he'd bought her a gift touched her, even if it was practical. She couldn't recall the last gift she'd received. It struck her as strange that something nice was happening just as something horrible overshadowed her life. "I need to go. I'm meeting someone tonight. Someone who may be able to offer advice that will help me."

"Do you want me to come with you?"

Eilidh smiled at Munro, and he smiled back. Maybe she *could* have a friend. She couldn't let herself think of anything more, no matter what her heart wanted.

"No, I'm sorry. I wish you could join me, but I need to move quickly and silently, and the faerie I'm meeting will not appear if he senses a human nearby. Our people are taught not to mix with humans. It is very deeply ingrained."

"So I noticed," he said and smiled again, although he appeared disappointed at her refusal.

She didn't quite know how to say goodbye. Humans shook hands or kissed, but she didn't feel comfortable with either. Among the fae, excessive touching was not done, even between friends. But Munro saved her from having to think on it further by simply opening the door. "Tell me how it goes then?"

She nodded and stepped outside and down the path. "I will."

He waved and shut the door.

She could not help but sigh with relief. She enjoyed his company, but she found houses overwhelming. All the trapped scents bothered her, and she felt walled off from the earth. She hadn't needed to leave quite yet. She had plenty of time before she met her father at the folly. But she needed to eat and didn't want to turn down Munro's inevitable offer of strange-smelling human food. And she knew Munro wasn't ready to watch her hunt. She loped through the city, going unnoticed out of habit. When she crossed the River Tay and headed toward the hills, her mouth started to water as she thought of the fresh rabbit she would have for dinner.

∞

The appointed hour was the darkest of the night. Imire had chosen the time when the kingdom borders were largest, so the shifting boundaries would move closer to the city and encompass the folly. Imire would not have to endure the discomfort of leaving the kingdom, and Eilidh would have an easy means of escape to the city, should things go wrong.

She sat cross-legged on the ancient stone table in front of the folly, a scant few feet from the edge of the cliff. The city sprawled below her. The ribbon-like River Tay ran alongside its northern curve. Lights from houses and tiny cars inched along the highway at the bottom of the sheer drop.

She had eaten, bathed in the river, and tried to prepare herself to see her father. But instead of anticipating their reunion, all she could think about was the fifty thousand humans who called Perth home. She was their only chance against a dark faerie, and she felt woefully ill-equipped. How could she fight something she didn't understand? She didn't even understand her own talent for the Path of the Azure. How could she come to grips with an ability so much darker and well-practiced than her own? The determination was there, but she didn't know where to start.

She felt Imire approach long before she heard or saw him. He unmasked his magic and let his presence flow gently ahead. She'd prepared what she would say and how she would behave. The meeting would be as difficult for him as for her. To make things easier, she would tell him she was well and happy and make him believe it at all costs. She would lay out her fears of the dark faerie methodically. He would *have* to see the dangers and at least try to convince the conclave to change their minds and act.

These thoughts disappeared when Imire walked up the path and she saw him for the first time in twenty-five years. She stood and approached him, taking in everything about his appearance. He wore the dark green robes he'd always favoured, but his frame was thinner and his face more drawn. His hair had gone from brilliant white to a dull grey, and his skin had lost its sheen.

The change shocked Eilidh. Imire was not yet seven hundred, and yet he looked like he approached his second millennium. It was because of her and her warped magical talents, because of her crimes and exile. If he'd let her be executed, it would at least have been over. Instead, he sacrificed his prime for her.

Without a word, Eilidh rushed to him, embracing him tightly as cool tears ran rivulets down her cheeks. "Father," she said. "You came."

He coughed his surprise and chuckled. "It's good to see you too, Eilidh. I was astonished to learn you stayed nearby." He wistfully added, "All this time. I'd imagined you were far away, maybe even over the seas."

As a child, she'd heard stories from fae who travelled. She'd learned there were many kingdoms throughout the world, all connected through the Otherworld, but each with a different earthly presence. Not once had she thought to seek out those other kingdoms. She opened her mouth to explain why she hadn't left, but now she wasn't sure. How could she say that she'd stayed simply because she hadn't gone? Here, she knew the dangers, the likely places of influence, where she could safely hunt, where to find water and shelter. The population of humans was small, the air clean, the water pure.

Finally, Imire released her and held her at arm's length. "You look tired, daughter." He glanced over her clothes and her new black knitted cap, which covered her ears and her white hair.

She didn't acknowledge his true meaning. Instead, she said, "The blood faerie has killed again. This time he failed to preserve the heart. I encountered him last night." She gestured to the stone table, and they sat together. "Father, he is so strong. He is practiced in the Path of the Azure, and I cannot defeat him alone."

"Why do you feel it necessary to defeat him? Is he your enemy? Has he harmed you?"

Eilidh blinked. "He has killed two already. There may be others I do not know of. I only know of these deaths because they happened in my city."

"Your city?" Imire smiled. "They were human deaths. Tragic, perhaps, and grotesque, certainly, but what are they to you?"

The pleasure at seeing her father faltered, and she stared at his aging face in disbelief. "I am their Watcher," she said finally. "They have no other."

"Do they know you exist?"

Had he called her here just to tell her humans were not worth saving? He, who had possibly never spoken to a human? "Evil must be challenged, Father." She turned back to the city. She knew that many fae would consider *her* evil, for the mere fact that she'd been born with a talent for the Path of the Azure, an addictive, powerful, and manipulative magic. But she didn't think her father was one of those.

He clasped his hand over hers. He may have aged, but he still held power. "Yes, it must." A smile spread across his face, and she could tell it was an unaccustomed expression. "There are so many things I wish I could have taught you. I did my best, but I just didn't have enough time."

"I'm sorry, Father." The tears threatened to fall again. "For all of it."

"My child, the fault is not yours, but mine. It is only my own pride and fear of losing even this one precious moment that I do not confess to you how deeply my guilt runs."

He had known. The thought froze Eilidh in place. When? All her life? From before she was born? As she opened her mouth to ask the hundred questions that flooded her mind, he said, "I can do a small thing, perhaps, to make up for it. I do not pretend to think it will compensate for all, but perhaps it will ease your pain somewhat."

A cool breeze dried the tears on her cheeks. She hadn't even heard him call the wind.

"I have travelled far, these past decades, searching for some clue that would be of help to you. I spoke to every faerie who would listen, in the Otherworld and the three kingdoms of Europe."

Eilidh hesitated. Her father *travelled*? She had never known him to leave his study out of choice, much less the kingdom.

"The fae laugh easily and avoid the darkness. It occurred to me that we are a frivolous people. I have always loved my books and I never thought too closely on the subject. Until you left, I didn't see the truth. But we are shallow and vain, Eilidh. Shallow and vain." He sighed.

"What did you seek?"

"Peace, I suppose. Forgiveness? A way to make restitution."

Eilidh smiled at the familiar, wandering patterns of her father's thoughts. "And what did you find?"

"In the past millennium, seventy-five faeries have been executed or exiled from the three kingdoms of Europe. Sixty-one for following the Path of the

Azure. Fifty are dead." His voice caught. "Fifty," he repeated.

Eilidh understood his pain at voicing the number. Faerie children were rare, and their numbers dwindled as the human influence grew. More and more didn't even want to enter the human realm, but it was only through the human realm the fae had the power to reproduce. Children were a gift from the Great Mother of the Earth. Fae who remained in the Otherworld would live much longer, but remain childless forever. To lose fifty fae children, even over so long a span, seemed unthinkable.

"Of the eleven others," he said, breaking the thoughtful silence, "one is, of course, you. Of the other ten, I heard many rumours, and it's difficult to sift fact from myth." He gave Eilidh a smile that begged indulgence. "You know how we fae like our stories and legends." Usually, those legends found their way into epic poems, chants, or songs. Eilidh doubted very much anyone would ever sing songs about *her*.

Continuing, he said, "But one story kept coming up. A story of three faeries, cast out in the early days of the Magical Amendment. The details change...their names, their ages, their crimes, but one place is mentioned in nearly every story: *Eilean a' Cheò*."

"The Isle of Skye? Why did you search for this information for so long, and why are you telling me about this now? Do you think they could help me fight against this dark faerie?" She considered. It would be invaluable to have three more fae by her side—and elder fae at that.

"That I do not know."

"Then why?"

"Because they can do what I never could. They can teach you. Unless you develop your power, you have no hope of stopping the evil this blood faerie brings to your city." Imire squeezed her hand again. "If it were not for the edict forbidding any from aiding you in your quest, I would be tempted to fight him myself."

"The conclave made an edict?"

He nodded, and a flash of anger marred his face. "They are fools. They actually believe you are trying to draw us out of the protection of the kingdom lands."

"What? Why would I do that?"

Imire shrugged. "Revenge, perhaps? They have grown brittle in their minds." He paused. "I would fight, but the edict is not the only reason. And not all of them are fools. Some believe you mean well and think the dark faerie should be watched. I hope to work with them, to educate them of the things I have learned in my travels. But if I went against the will of the conclave, their hearts would be hardened against you, and our people would suffer in ignorance."

"I understand." In truth, hearing his explanation did make her feel better. She didn't hold out hope that the conclave would change its mind, but it was good to know not all thought her an evil monster.

"I have asked Saor to go with you." Imire gestured toward the trees, and Saor stepped forward. He bowed respectfully to Imire and gave Eilidh a formal nod.

"To Skye? But what about the edict?"

Saor spread his hands and gave an innocent smile. "There is no edict saying I cannot travel, only that I cannot investigate directly the claims you have made about the blood shadows. If we happen to travel in the same direction, who can say it is anything but coincidence? I have been tied to the borders and my duties as a Watcher for a long time. Many have urged me to go on a retreat. What better place than one known to hold so many stones for communion with the Mother?"

"Few know of the stories I have told you about, Eilidh. Saor will be safe from recriminations."

"Why do you think I need an escort? I was a Watcher myself. I still am, of a sort. I am no longer a child."

"Indulge me? Just this one last time?"

Eilidh glanced at Saor, who watched impassively, then into her father's eyes. "Of course, Father. I owe you at least that. You gave me life and then saved it, even though it cost you much."

Imire stood and looked at the stars. "The night is waning."

Eilidh nodded. When the sun rose, the kingdom influence would retreat from this place, and her father would lose the magic and protection of the Otherworld. But an idea struck her, and she couldn't lose this chance to ask him a question that pressed in her mind. "Have you ever encountered a human with power?"

He stopped and peered at her. "What sort of power?" His eyebrows narrowed and his expression became serious.

"Affinity with the Ways of Earth. The power to shape stone with his hands, to speak through stone." Her eyes flicked to Saor, who also had begun to pay rapt attention.

"Can he speak the incantation? Does he see the flows?" Imire's voice grew excited, the way it did when he discovered a scroll everyone thought had been lost.

"I don't know."

"Is this the one you've grown so *close* to?" Saor asked. He couldn't keep the disgusted sneer from his voice.

Annoyance grew in Eilidh. "He is a *friend*. The only friend I have," she said coldly.

Imire didn't acknowledge the tension between Saor and Eilidh. His eyes darted back and forth as though he was reading something in his head. "A true druid? Could it be?" he muttered. His eyes came into focus and he gripped Eilidh's hand firmly, pulling her close to him. "Can you bring him to me?"

"Perhaps. I'll ask him. I'm not certain how he would feel about it. He still seems confused, but I know he has the affinity."

"You must bind him to you," Imire said. "That's the only way."

"Bind him? The only way for what?" Eilidh grew more concerned at the feverish excitement on her father's face.

"Go to Skye. They'll teach you how."

"Teach me how to what?"

Imire seemed to have regained his composure somewhat and he paused and straightened, patting her hand gently. "Go to Skye. I cannot teach you this. It's in the Path of the Azure."

Eilidh nodded, but for some reason she didn't trust the gleam in her father's eyes. Bind Quinton? Whatever her father wanted her to do, she had to tread carefully. But if it would hold answers for herself and for Quinton, she must indeed go to Skye. She only hoped she would not be gone long and that the blood faerie would not kill while she was away.

CHAPTER 11

MUNRO FELT EILIDH'S PRESENCE long before he pulled into the drive. It didn't compel him the way it had when he'd been so feverish. Feeling her presence was like closing his eyes and being able to tell where the sun was in the sky. She was a warmth in his mind. He found that he knew where she went throughout the day, at least in which direction. He often wondered how far away she was and why she travelled from one place to another. Was she investigating the deaths, or did she have other friends and other things to do? He knew so little about her. When he parked his car, he wasn't surprised to feel her inside his house, but he did wonder why and how she'd gotten inside.

He didn't become wary until he heard her voice and realised she hadn't come alone. "See," she was saying. "You have to wait a moment for it to happen, but the red dot water becomes hot. Feel it. They don't even have to call fire." Munro could hear the kitchen taps being turned on and off repeatedly.

Then someone opened the refrigerator. "And it stays cold in here all the time. So meats don't spoil as quickly."

A man's voice answered, "That's ridiculous. Why don't they just smoke their meat?"

"Maybe they don't like smoked meat? But look at that. That's milk."

"Cold milk? How could you drink it cold?"

"I think they heat it up in this heating machine first."

"But if they just got it straight from the goat, they wouldn't have to make it cold and then make it hot later. It's a waste of time. I never realised what a burden all of these machines would be."

Munro stood in the doorway, watching the two faeries peer into his fridge as though it was the strangest thing they'd ever seen. He didn't know whether to laugh or be annoyed that they'd broken in. "Eilidh?" he said finally.

He might have expected her to be abashed at having been caught, but instead she seemed smug. The other faerie managed to look superior, aghast, and bemused all at the same time. Munro disliked him instantly. If Eilidh had an ethereal presence about her, this guy did doubly so. He had straight golden hair that hung down his back and skin that was more yellow-gold than tan. His clothing was definitely not from any shop Munro knew. The faerie wore kidskin trousers that fit his long legs perfectly and a flowing woven shirt of a green so dark it looked nearly black. The faerie was taller than Eilidh and easily reached Munro's own height.

"Quinton," she said, "This is Saor. He was a friend of mine. He will escort me to Skye."

Was? Munro ignored the introduction and the flicker of annoyance that crossed Saor's face when Munro did not return his bow. "To Skye?" Munro said to Eilidh. "You're going to bloody Skye? When?"

"Tonight. I wanted to speak with you before we left."

Slightly mollified that at least she thought to tell him she was going, he turned his attention to Saor and nodded. "Nice to meet you," he said, not really meaning it. "So are you an exile too?"

Saor narrowed his eyes. "Certainly not." Despite the awkward moment, the faerie held out a bundle of sticks with both hands. "For your hearth," he said.

Munro would have thought it a useless gift, not to mention a strange one, but he felt something about the sticks that he couldn't quite place. He didn't know what they did, but he could tell they weren't ordinary twigs. "Thank you," he said gruffly.

Eilidh stepped forward and guided Munro to the living room. "You are vexed with me," she said quietly as they walked, "but I do not understand why. Have I done something wrong again?"

She stood, holding his arm, blinking at him with those swirling silver eyes, and he couldn't be annoyed. "I'm surprised you're going is all. How did you get in the house anyway?" He didn't know what the sticks were for, so he didn't know where to put them that wouldn't be offensive. So he stuck them in the middle of the living room table. He'd ask Eilidh about them later.

"Through the door." She tilted her head. "Isn't that the usual way?"

He chuckled. "I locked it."

"Oh!" she said. "I thought the lock was to keep out human thieves, not friends." She glanced at Saor, who had followed them. "Should we have waited outside?"

Munro started to say yes, but imagined what the neighbours would have said if these two had sat on his doorstep for any length of time. "It's fine. Just unexpected." He'd work out a way to tell her he didn't mind her so much, but if she was bringing friends, she really should ask. Since she was leaving town that night, it could wait, he supposed. Besides, he didn't want to say anything in front of this smug faerie bastard she'd brought with her. He was just so damned arrogant. "Why Skye? And why now?"

Munro sat down, and the faeries followed suit. Eilidh told him she'd met with her father, taking care to impress upon Munro how dangerous and unusual it was for her father to risk meeting with her. Munro took it to mean it was equally unusual for her to see Saor, although it was obvious they had some kind of connection. They looked closely at each other and gave subtle nods, as if they could read each other's thoughts. Eilidh went on to explain that her father believed she might find help among three faeries who lived in Skye. Interestingly, it was obvious Saor did not approve of her giving away certain details. He seemed to want to protect any information about the fae and where they lived—even the outcasts.

"Why are you going, Saor?" Munro wanted to know.

"To watch over Eilidh."

"Eilidh seems like she can take care of herself." Munro didn't want to admit he was glad Eilidh wouldn't be on her own, but he certainly didn't like the idea of her going away with this guy.

Eilidh smiled her approval at Munro. It made his heart melt in a way he didn't welcome. She'd made her feelings clear, but when she looked at him like that, he believed he could do anything.

"I voiced the same argument to my father, Quinton, but he asked me to go with Saor, and I couldn't deny him."

Saor looked at Munro pointedly. "I was the natural choice. Eilidh and I were once promised to one another."

He was unmistakably staking out his territory, but Munro didn't want to make it easy for him. "But not anymore." His inflection landed somewhere between a question and a statement.

"No," Eilidh agreed. "Not anymore."

Saor slipped his hand over Eilidh's. She seemed surprised at the gesture, but she didn't take her hand away. "I will always be concerned for Eilidh's welfare."

Munro ignored it as best he could. He had to find a way to keep his mind on the job at hand. He took off his jacket, tossed it across the back of a chair, and sighed. Work had been mundane, and he hadn't gotten anywhere near the murder cases, except to ferret out the latest gossip.

The two faeries waited patiently while Munro made himself more comfortable. He scrubbed his hand through his short hair. Eilidh was going away. He needed her. *For the case*, he told himself as quickly as the thought had formed. And she was going away to Skye, for fuck's sake. With this…other faerie. He didn't like it, but he could see the logic in it. She didn't believe they could stop this blood faerie alone, so it made sense to ask for help. "When are you coming back?"

"Soon," she said, smiling as though she could read his conflicted emotions.

Damn. He had no idea what *soon* meant to her, but he supposed it was all he could ask for.

"Quinton," Eilidh said. "The reason I wanted to speak to you before we left is that I asked my father some questions concerning your abilities."

"My what?" He knew what she was saying, but he stalled anyway. He really hadn't given it more thought and instead just accepted that he could tell where Eilidh was all the time. The thing where he felt the life in the stone at the church and shaped the small rock? It hadn't happened again, so he put it out of his mind, assuming it had to do with Eilidh and not him.

"My father thinks you may be a druid," she said.

"A *true* druid," Saor added, as though that actually explained anything.

Munro laughed. "Aren't those the guys that dance around at Stonehenge?" When both faeries stared at him blankly he added, "The circle of standing stones?"

The glance that passed between the pair spoke volumes. They didn't seem familiar with the word *Stonehenge*, but they knew exactly what the standing stones were. Of course, there were a couple dozen or more sites of ancient standing stones in Scotland alone. He never paid them any mind beyond a passing curiosity. They suddenly took on new possible meanings when he thought of them in terms of the faerie world, of which he knew nothing.

"I do not know exactly what their practices are," Eilidh said. "Although I am still quite young, having just passed my first century mark twenty years ago, I can say that I have never encountered a true druid before you. My father says it has to do with the Path of the Azure, the practice of which was outlawed by my people a thousand years ago during the Magical Amendment."

She's a hundred and twenty years old? Damn. Munro nodded, but he really didn't understand what this meant for him, if anything. It was hard to imagine himself as having abilities, as she put it. "Nothing happens except when you're around. I just assumed it was you."

Eilidh shook her head. "I am not strong in the Ways of Earth, and stone is my weakest element. I could not do the things you suggest." She paused for a moment. "Is there no one in your family with strange abilities? Although our spheres of influence are granted by the Mother and do not run in bloodlines, our strength often does. It would make sense for yours to do the same."

Saor stared at Munro, as though catching him in an untruth. "Stone is my primary strength. Show me."

Munro shrugged. "I don't know how."

Eilidh said, "The rock. The one you shaped. Do you still have it?"

He nodded and went to his bedroom to get it. When he came back, he handed it to Saor and sat down again. "I don't know how it happened. Like I said, I thought Eilidh did it."

Saor turned the rock over in his hand and whispered to it. Munro saw a flicker in the grey surface that quickly dissipated. Saor met his eyes. "Find another piece of stone and bring it to me."

"I don't really have anything stone that I can think of."

"Metal?"

"I'm sure there's something. Does it matter what kind of metal?"

"No, any object of earth will show me what I need to see."

As he stood to do as Saor asked, Munro noted that the male faerie still seemed as arrogant and smug as before, but now he appeared interested. Munro went to the kitchen. He didn't want to take Saor something valuable because he didn't know what the faerie was going to do with it. He dug around in a utility drawer and found an old padlock that had once been on his father's shed. Somewhere along the line, Munro lost the key, so the thing was stuck closed. He didn't know why he'd kept it, but he couldn't throw it away. Then again, his dad wouldn't have approved of being sentimental over something as silly as an old padlock. Munro plucked it out of the drawer and took it to Saor.

The faerie set Munro's stone teardrop on the table and took the lock. "A simple mechanism," he muttered to himself. He held it between his hands and within a few seconds the u-shaped shackle disengaged from the body of the lock with a loud click. Munro shook his head. That explained how the two of them got into his house so easily.

Saor handed it to Munro. "Did you see the flows?"

"I'm not sure," Munro said. "I saw a spark before, when you touched the teardrop, but the lock happened too fast. I wasn't paying attention."

Saor snorted with disgust. "We can hardly help you if you are going to let your mind wander like a child. I suppose by our standards, you are a child."

Munro refused to rise to the bait. He snapped the lock closed to see if he could do what Saor had done. He tried to focus on the metal, but it seemed so unyielding that it didn't want to bend to his thoughts. He sighed. "I don't think it was me that did those things, Eilidh." He held the lock in his hand and thought about his dad. How the old man would have laughed to see his son trying to open a lock with magic.

"It's all right, Quinton. It may take some time." Eilidh gave Saor a pointed look. "Even a fae child has to learn over many years to master the flows."

Munro liked Eilidh comparing him to a child even less than he liked Saor doing it, but he could hardly argue. She was a hundred and twenty bloody years old.

"If," Saor said, "he has any talent at all."

Eilidh pointed to the teardrop. "What of this then?"

Saor shrugged with perfect nonchalance. "Maybe he's right. Maybe it was your influence. None of us truly understand your affinity with the Path of the Azure."

Eilidh frowned, but didn't contradict him. Instead, she stood and Saor rose with her. "I'll find out what I can and be back with all haste. I don't know if these faeries will help us, or what they can teach me. But if we're going to stop these killings, this is the best chance we have."

Munro nodded and stood to show them to the door. They left with little ceremony. He assumed saying goodbye was not a fae tradition, because they simply walked out when the conversation ended. He found it disconcerting on one hand, but on the other, he liked not having to find the right thing to say to Eilidh. He wanted to tell her to hurry back, to stay safe, but he couldn't ask her to do either of those things, not if it compromised what she needed to do.

He locked the front door and slid the deadbolt shut. Neither action made him feel better, considering how easily Saor opened the padlock. He couldn't help but wonder if the blood faerie had the same talent. The thought certainly didn't make him rest any easier.

Munro felt surprisingly tired, considering he'd just had a couple days off work. Part of him worried about another seizure, but nothing had happened since then and he'd managed to go through the motions at work without any bother. In light of that, he decided on a bowl of soup and an early night.

When he went to the kitchen, he realised he'd been carrying the padlock around with him the whole time. He opened the junk drawer and tossed it in with the other remnants he couldn't be bothered to deal with: rubber bands, the microwave oven instruction manual, duct tape, a box of nails, and dozens of other odds and ends. It wasn't until he went to shut the drawer that he noticed the padlock was no longer a padlock. The metal had twisted and fused together in his hand. The shape was roughly hewn, but unmistakably that of a miniature grizzly bear, standing on its haunches, its head thrown back in a roar.

Munro picked it up and turned it over. It had the same weight as before, but it seemed to have been moulded as a child would shape clay. He glanced toward the front door. He wanted to call Eilidh back, to show her what he'd done and ask all the questions he should have asked a half hour ago. But she was long gone, and he was on his own.

∞

In the following two days, Munro found out what the Dewer task force had learned from the second crime scene. He'd been asked to help canvas the Muirton area for more witnesses. Part of him feared someone would remember seeing him and Eilidh that night. He needn't have worried though, because nobody seemed to have seen much of anything.

One of the other teams discovered what they thought was something of interest. The Tayside Harriers, a local athletics group, regularly used the track behind the school. Several of the members reported seeing a couple of men hanging about for several hours. They were there when the athletes arrived for their semi-weekly training and were still hanging around when the athletes left a couple of hours later. That's what had made them stand out. It sent the task force into a bit of a tizzy. It was certainly unusual, but what bothered everyone was that neither man fit the description of the latest victim. They started to ask if it was possible two men had been involved in the crimes.

Serial killers were rare. Much rarer than most people thought. Scotland only had two confirmed serial killers he knew of in the past century. As far as serial killers working in pairs, Munro learned that male/male was the most common pairing, but it bothered him to see the task force going in a direction he knew was false. This wasn't the work of a typical anti-social, abused-as-a-child loner or even a dysfunctional pair, but he couldn't exactly tell them the truth. All he could do was keep his ears open. If nothing else, being close to the case might give him something that could lead him and Eilidh to find the blood faerie.

Munro could feel Eilidh somewhere in the distance. She had gone so far he couldn't tell anything more than a vague direction. If he didn't know better, he'd likely not notice the compulsion to glance northwest a few times a day.

He couldn't get what she'd said out of his head. He didn't understand it all, but obviously Eilidh thought he had some kind of abilities. The stone teardrop and the metal bear told him something had changed in him, but he didn't know what. He thought about Eilidh's question about his family. Could he have inherited the ability? His parents had been so normal. Granted, he'd been quite young when his mum died, but he'd surely remember something like turning padlocks into bears.

The only real family he had left was his Aunt Judith over in Scone. He needed to get out of the house anyway. In the evenings, when he went home, he spent his time thinking about the case, wondering when the blood faerie would strike again. When he wasn't doing that, he was wondering about Eilidh and if she was having any success in Skye. So now seemed as good a time as any to pay a visit to Aunt Judith. She'd be surprised and probably guess that something was up, but he assured himself he'd think of an excuse.

He dropped in on her that night, and she filled him full of tea and Battenberg sponge cake. If, at any point in the evening, she'd sussed out that he wanted particular information on family magical ability, she didn't let on.

"You wait here, love. Let me go get that album. The one with photos of your mum and dad." She seemed pleased to talk about family and the past. Her small, round face lit up as she spoke about Munro's parents.

She returned with an armful of ancient albums with vinyl covers and yellowing plastic sheets protecting the pictures. They went over each photo, Judith lost in reminiscing about his mum and dad, then her own husband Harold, who'd also passed on. When the conversation turned to her kids, he found his eyes glazing over a little, although he did make an effort to be polite.

"Young Carol is pregnant again," Judith said. Young Carol was Judith's daughter, and she must have been in her mid-thirties. Everyone in the family still called her Young Carol though, because she was named after Judith's own Aunt Carol. "She's working for one of the local councils near Edinburgh still."

"Oh, really? Tell her I send my best wishes," Munro said.

"You could pick up the phone and tell her yourself," Judith replied with a hint of scolding. Munro gave a shrug that showed he was duly chastised, and they moved on to talk about Judith's older son Raymond, who worked in a bank. Judith couldn't have been more proud. But that she didn't mention her youngest, Frankie, made Munro take notice. After hearing one more story than he thought he could stand about how marvellous Young Carol's children were, Munro politely asked about Frankie.

Judith tutted. It was a small noise, but it spoke volumes. Munro hadn't really kept up with his cousins. The older two had moved away, and although Frankie didn't live that far, it hadn't seemed like they had much in common. They saw each other on Boxing Day or New Year's at Judith's when Munro didn't have to work, but ever since his dad died, Munro found excuses to miss family events.

"Is Frankie not well?" Munro asked.

"I tried with him," Judith finally relented and said. "Lord knows, I tried."

After some gentle probing, something Munro did every day at work, Judith revealed that Frankie turned out to be a bit of a disappointment. He'd dropped out of university in the first term, which Munro vaguely remembered hearing some years before. That had been a blow to her, but then he'd not taken up much of a trade. She encouraged him to try to get an apprenticeship, but he ended up working in a local video store during the day and spending his nights with "some band".

"He'd always been quite good on the drums," Munro offered.

She rolled her eyes and went on a familiar tirade about how his Uncle Harold had converted their garage to a sound-proof room, only to have Frankie and his mates spend more time practicing elsewhere.

"It's not just the music though," Judith confided with a tired sigh.

"No?"

"I always wondered if he was a bit touched in the head. I shouldn't say it. Harold wouldn't like it, I can promise you that. But he just isn't like the rest of us. He has a funny way."

That didn't really say anything about Frankie being magical or not, but "touched in the head" was probably how Aunt Judith would describe a druid, to be fair. Munro finally left amidst promises of coming by more often and definitely making Boxing Day this year. He promised he'd give Carol a call too. But he couldn't shake the sense that he should get in touch with Frankie. He couldn't imagine Carol or Raymond the banker were true druids, but Eilidh hadn't given him much to go on.

It seemed a long shot, and Munro wasn't sure what he hoped to gain. But if magical abilities ran in bloodlines, and someone in his family tree could explain what was going on, it would be worth making a bit of an idiot of himself to find out. He'd start with Frankie. If that proved to be a waste of time, he could hop down to Edinburgh over the weekend to see Carol or Raymond next.

CHAPTER 12

EILIDH AND SAOR DID the sensible thing. They stayed close to the roads, but tried to avoid traffic. Saor, still attuned to fae nocturnal habits and not comfortable away from the healing essence of the Otherworld, let his path diverge from Eilidh's a few times. She also knew he would sometimes wander into the forests alone at night, while she slept near a roadside restaurant or car park. It wasn't comfortable and it didn't smell nice, but the further north they went, the human settlements grew more sparse and gaps in the kingdom territories grew fewer. Saor argued that they should move at night for that very reason. He didn't want to sleep when they would be most vulnerable. Eilidh pointed out that their passage through the territories would be more likely to be noticed at night. They compromised by only stopping for a couple of hours at a time.

Saor was unhappy about sticking to the roads because of the smells and the added distance, but he had less reason to be cautious. *He* didn't have a death sentence hanging over his head. Even though the fae had much stronger constitutions than humans and slept less, the trip wearied Eilidh. She was not accustomed to keeping the incredibly fast pace. In her church tower, she often dreamed of running through the highlands the way she and Saor had done during their childhood. But the time away from her homeland had taken its toll. Running two hundred miles tired her in a way it wouldn't have thirty years earlier.

Saor was aloof, and she could tell he had something on his mind beyond his annoyance at the human encroachment into fae territory. The fae didn't own property, of course, not in the way humans did. They did, however, respect certain boundaries, especially those created by the ebb and flow of magical mists from the Otherworld.

He didn't share what was bothering him until they stopped for the last time before approaching the Isle of Skye. They'd run for days, sometimes having to go long distances out of their way to avoid a cluster of fae or an Otherworld gateway. Once they got to the smaller roads, the lands were awash in fae magic, and there was no longer anywhere to hide. Even the human homes dotted around were not enough to disrupt the flows.

Eilidh had grown more uncomfortable with each passing mile. Saor watched well, and his affinity for the earth helped him sense even the delicate footsteps of any fae within a quarter mile. The extra expenditure of energy tired him though, and the strain of worry made Eilidh snappish and edgy. She was surrounded now. If they were caught, she had little hope of escape.

When they stopped near the village of Eilanreach for the night, their last rest before crossing the sound, Saor went into the woods to hunt. He returned later with a brace of rabbits, which he dropped at Eilidh's feet, before walking to a nearby stream to wash. There was a time when she would have joined him, and they would have laughed and played in the water. Now she averted her eyes and focused on skinning their dinner.

At least he had dressed before returning to camp. When he continued to exude displeasure with her, she asked, "Why did you come?"

He shrugged lightly. "Imire made a reasonable request."

She shook her head. "That isn't the reason."

"Once, you would not have asked me that."

"Once," she replied, "I was a kingdom faerie. Now I am an exile, and you could be punished for aiding me."

"Perhaps things can change."

"What things? The conclave will not lift the death sentence. You know that. It is not in their nature to be tolerant or forgiving."

"You said yourself you do not cast the azure."

Eilidh frowned. "Even with what happened, the *incident* that brought my nature to light, my crime was not casting the azure. You know that, Saor. It was being *able* to." She wondered what had caused his anger to melt and be replaced by this strange new passion.

"We do not punish faeries who have violence in their hearts, only those who commit wrong acts." A long silence stretched between them. Finally, he added, "When you left, I thought I'd never see you again. I grieved for you, and I tried to put it behind me. But I never could. You were meant for me. Everyone knew that."

"You think if I vowed never to cast the azure, the conclave would believe me? This choice was not offered to me twenty-five years ago. Why would it be now?" She wanted to laugh and dismiss the thought, but Saor's seriousness gave her pause.

"If they would not believe your solemn vow, you could offer to be severed."

Severed? To endure a magical process so harsh, so painful? To never be capable of touching any magic, even the Ways of Earth, again? To never see a flow or sense the outer reaches of the Halls of Mist? In that state she could never enter the Otherworld, but would be forever confined to the earthly reaches of the fae kingdom. The idea stunned her. No one would ever volunteer for such a thing. It would be considered a fate worse than death. The fae breathed magic. They *were* magic. To separate a faerie from magic was to cleave them from life.

Eilidh could feel him waiting for her response. Words escaped her. In all her years, it never occurred to her. Any fae would sooner pluck out their own eyes than offer to be severed. Even if it were possible, would she make that ultimate sacrifice? Would it be any better than living in exile? She would have her father back, and Saor, it seemed, but would other faeries accept her? For decades she would have given anything to return to her old life, but to go back like that? Completely crippled in her soul?

"It's possible," Saor said, "if we do find these faeries who know the Path of the Azure, that they will determine your astral gifts are as weak as your talents in the Ways of Earth."

"So weak," Eilidh said, "that I wouldn't be any threat, or that I wouldn't mind being severed?"

"Perhaps."

So *this* was why he wanted to come. Not to help her untap her powers and receive training and not to ask for help in defeating the blood faerie. Instead, he hoped they would find her abilities so weak they would not be worth exploring, to find some reassurance that would cause the conclave to stop viewing her as a threat.

When she didn't reply, Saor's frustration came to the surface. "You're thinking of *him*, aren't you? That human. You've convinced yourself he's some kind of druid from a book of fables to make him more acceptable to you. After all, what's the difference between a weak faerie and a strong human?"

It felt like he'd slapped her. His anger shocked her and stirred her own ire. "You do not want me to have friends, Saor? You can't stand to be near my deformed magic, so you would rather see me stripped of it than to see me whole and happy?"

Saor's eyes glowed with fire. "Are you saying you're happy with him?"

"You're jealous." Even though his whole demeanour was infuriating, it touched her to see how much he still cared, that he still wanted her.

"Of a human? Don't be ridiculous."

She sat in silence for a few moments, letting their tempers cool. "This plan of yours, I don't know that the conclave would even consider it. You know how they are."

"But would *you* consider it? To have your life back? To have *us* back?" It struck her, suddenly, how beautiful he was. His expression was fiercer and more passionate than she'd ever seen it. When she didn't answer at first, he stepped in close and kissed her tenderly on the lips. He tasted of honey. She'd forgotten how sweet his kisses were, and it made her ache. "Saor..." she began, but she didn't know how to finish. Could she do what he wanted?

He silenced her with another kiss and then reached up and removed the black hat from her head. He ran a finger along her left ear, sending shivers down her spine. "Just think on what I've said, Eilidh. We belong together." He glanced at the sky. "We should rest for a while and swim the sound at first light. I don't want to approach these outcasts during full dark."

Eilidh nodded, too stunned by Saor's words and actions to say anything. She lay on the ground in a bed of heather, but she could not close her eyes, much less sleep. She watched the stars move overhead in their slow dance across the night sky.

∞

Even by the time Munro found himself on his cousin Frankie's doorstep, he hadn't yet worked out what he would say. *Hi, cousin. So, can you do magic?* He settled on playing things by ear, but he hadn't been able to fool himself into thinking he'd suddenly come up with something that wouldn't sound barmy.

He approached the house and took the two steps up to the front door. When he rang the bell, he got no answer. Music drifted from the other side of the house, though, and he decided to peek around back. Sure enough, the sound of heavy metal reverberated from the garage.

Munro didn't have to knock, because the side door stood wide open and the waft of paint fumes drifted into the yard. He hardly recognised his cousin beneath the safety mask and goggles, bent over an old sanded-down wheel arch with a can of spray paint, but the shock of black hair couldn't be anyone else's. Munro waited for Frankie to see him, since knocking or calling out wouldn't be heard over the banging music. Just as the song wound down, Frankie looked up. When his cousin removed his mask and goggles, he greeted Munro with a smile.

"Well, if it isn't Eastwood, come to visit."

Munro laughed. No one had called him Eastwood in years. Not since school. Quinton had been shortened to Quint, which morphed into Clint, which became Eastwood, after the Hollywood actor. As nicknames went, it could have been worse.

Munro nodded hello and pointed to the wheel arch. "Where's the rest of it?"

Frankie grinned. "Belongs to a friend who got into a bit of a scrape." He thought a minute and then laughed at his own pun. He wiped his hands on a rag and tossed it aside. "Let's chat in the house. It's a bit whiffy in here. Drink?"

"Sure," Munro said.

"Mum told me you stopped in to see her. Said you might be coming by."

"Did she? I got the impression you two don't talk much."

Frankie chuckled, leading Munro in through the back door and straight into the kitchen. He fetched two Cokes from the fridge and tossed one to Munro. "She moans about my music and my friends and my general worthlessness, but you know Mum, she doesn't mean it. She just likes to have a bit of a go at me sometimes." Frankie shrugged as though it didn't bother him in the least.

Munro tapped the can in his hand. "Since when did you give up beer?"

Frankie smiled. "As soon as the magic wouldn't let me drink anymore. Not everyone has that problem, but it does a number on my head."

Shock, excitement, and no small measure of relief made Munro stop cold. He stared for a moment while Frankie studied his face with amusement. Finally, Munro said, "At least I don't have to figure out how to ask."

Pointing toward the living room, Frankie said, "Let's sit. You look like you're about to faint." He patted Munro on the back. "I'm glad I'm not the only one any more though."

"So Carol and Raymond aren't…"

"No, just me. I got it from my dad, apparently. From what I've learned, girls can carry it, but they never have the abilities. So you got it from your mum, but you must have figured that out or you wouldn't be here."

"Not really," Munro said. "You're just one of the few family I have left." Was it dumb luck that brought him here, he wondered, or had he used the same ability that led him to Eilidh that day in the woods?

"Who unlocked you?"

"Who what?"

Frankie took a drink from his Coke, seeming to choose his next words carefully. "From what I've been taught, your abilities get unlocked by someone else. It takes a while to learn things. I'm not that strong yet, but I must be getting stronger. I could feel your magic as soon as you came into the garage." He grinned. "Sounds like a lot of woo-woo new age shite, doesn't it?"

Munro laughed. "Kind of does, yeah. Never would have believed it if I hadn't seen it for myself."

"So, who is your mentor? Might be someone I know." Something in Frankie's tone was guarded.

Munro could only assume he meant Eilidh. She was the only person he knew who had any kind of magical ability. *Mentor* would be taking it a bit far, but who else could Frankie mean? Munro hadn't planned to lie, but he didn't want to expose Eilidh. Just because Frankie knew about druids and magic didn't mean he knew about the fae. It didn't seem like Eilidh knew about other druids, so it stood to reason they weren't aware of her. "It just sort of happened. Started a couple of weeks ago."

Frankie frowned, but nodded. "Like I said, I'm not that strong. I've been practicing less than a year. I certainly don't know everything. So, what happened? Must've been something big if it unlocked you without a mentor."

Munro took a long drink, stalling. He'd been desperate to find some help, but now that he had it, he felt wary and uncertain about revealing too much. On the other hand, he couldn't see the harm in just talking about himself. He reached into his pocket and pulled out the stone tear and the bear. He set them on the table and watched as Frankie stared at them for a moment.

Frankie didn't touch them, but instead hovered his hand over the bear. "This one is fresher." He glanced at Munro for confirmation and then moved on. "You shaped these with the flows?"

"I guess," Munro said. "I didn't even know I was doing it."

"Stone," Frankie muttered. "Interesting."

"What does that mean?" Munro remembered Eilidh and Saor talking about the Ways of Earth and affinity with stone or whatnot, but they'd never fully explained it.

"We call our abilities earth magic. There are four spheres and they correspond to the seasons and elements. The first season is winter and the air element. Next is water and spring. Stone is the element for the third season, and if you could do this without even thinking, I'd guess that's where you're strongest. It doesn't mean a strong druid couldn't learn the others, but your abilities will probably be strongest in the summer, and working with stone or clay will come naturally to you. Maybe you unlocked without a mentor because we're so close to the height of summer. I really don't know."

"What's the fourth?"

"Fire. That's the rarest. I've only met one fire druid before." Frankie tapped the stone tear lightly, as if afraid of what it might do. "You say this started a couple of weeks ago?"

"Yeah, I was outside a church and I put my hand on the stone. I felt...strange. A little bit later, I picked up this rock and was just holding it. Next thing I know, it had become this."

"A church? Was it St Paul's?"

Munro went still. He'd intentionally not mentioned the name, because he knew Eilidh lived there, at least some of the time. But now he thought of it another way—as the site of the first murder. "It was, actually," he said. "How did you know? Is it special?"

Frankie waved it off. "Nah, I just remember another stone druid saying he felt some resonance there." He shook his empty Coke can. "Want another?"

"No thanks." Munro tried to act as natural as he could while still keeping an eye on Frankie as he went into the kitchen. His cousin was lying. He wouldn't say he had a nose for it, not like he had those hunches for violence, and it certainly wasn't tied to any ability. Cops got lied to every day of the week. It came with the job. After a while, they got a feel for it. It was something in the eyes and the body language. People either lied well or lied badly, depending on how often they did it. Frankie was obviously unaccustomed to thinking on his feet.

Munro tried to tease the lie out of the statement. It was possible, of course, that some stone druid had felt Eilidh's presence. He had certainly responded to her magic. It must have been Eilidh who unlocked him, although she didn't seem to realise she'd done it. Perhaps Frankie somehow knew of her existence and wanted to keep the information from Munro. She certainly didn't know Frankie, from what she'd said about druids, but there was more going on than Munro could work out.

On the other hand, it could be that some druid, maybe even Frankie himself, knew something about the murder. Could Eilidh have been wrong? Could the perpetrator have been a druid and not a faerie? Maybe she sensed the magic and not the race of the person casting it. He wanted to ask Frankie what he knew about blood magic. That certainly didn't fit into the tidy four-season scheme he'd just explained. But then, Eilidh had suggested she had abilities other than the normal earth magic. Could it be that druids could cast the azure too?

When Frankie came back, he didn't have another can in his hands. "Hey," he said, "I was thinking of going to meet some of my friends tonight, a couple of druids. They could probably answer some questions I can't. Want to come?"

There's even more of us? "Sure," Munro said. He needed answers, and now not just for himself, but to see what these people knew about the murders. He would have liked backup, but he couldn't exactly invite Getty along. Besides, all he planned to do was ask a few questions. His thoughts went to Eilidh. He wished she were with him. He could have used her knowledge and keen senses, wherever they were going. "I just need to phone in first. We're all on call lately." That was total BS, but Frankie wouldn't know that.

Munro called his own number and faked a conversation, leaving it recorded on his land-line voice mail. If anything happened, at least someone could find out where he'd gone. "PC Munro here." A pause. "Okay, that's fine." Another pause, pretending to listen. "That's fine. I'm at my cousin's in town. I'll check in again in a couple hours." Feeling like an idiot he added, "No problem, Sarge. I have my phone with me." He hung up, hoping he didn't sound as stupid as he felt.

"You're working those murders?"

Munro didn't make too much of the fact that Frankie connected the two deaths. Perth was the sort of place that almost never had an unexplained death. Although they'd kept some of the details out of the press, having two bodies found in public places with no arrests would be enough to make anyone assume something was going on. "Not really. They've got CID detectives for that. They're just making everyone work longer hours to have higher visibility. Gotta let the public think we're making progress." He shrugged and tried to look suitably annoyed. He also felt like a bit of an arse for suspecting his own cousin of being involved in a murder, but something was up. He'd learned long ago that being a little suspicious was never a bad thing.

CHAPTER 13

THE LONG JOURNEY AND WAKEFUL NIGHT left Eilidh on edge. In the Ways of Earth, she'd only had limited success with the first season, her strongest. Tomorrow would be the height of the third season, and she would have the least connection to her earth power than any other time of year. It left her feeling vulnerable and weak. When Saor told her he'd encountered a few fae on a hunt the night before, she realised how lucky they'd been.

After they crossed the sound and set foot on the Isle of Skye, Saor used his small talent with fire to dry and warm them before they proceeded. Eilidh could tell he was just as anxious as she. She'd had to live with the idea of having Path of the Azure magic ever since she accidentally cast an illusion that nearly killed one of her kinsmen.

He had believed he saw a white stag, rare even in the Otherworld, in the highland forests. It had surprised her as much as it did him.

She remembered controlling the beast like a puppet. She played with it, seeing what it could do. It didn't have limitations like something real would, but she couldn't make it do just anything. Trying to discover the rules, Eilidh made it jump in the air. It took great concentration for her to hold it off the ground, but she didn't understand why. It wasn't real, after all. Then her kinsman, Piedre, leapt out at the stag, hunting knife drawn. He fell nearly four hundred feet straight down. Neither saw the drop until it was too late. The angle at which the stag stood—up the mountainside from them—deceived their eyes completely. If a fall like that occured in the Otherworld, he would have survived with nothing more than a deep bruising to his pride. In the hills of Earth, though, even the fae were vulnerable to tragedy.

She could tell by his distance the idea of the Path of the Azure filled Saor with horror. As far as she knew, he'd never seen Eilidh cast it and seemed to be in some denial that it was real. As they walked inland, tension wracked his shoulders. He frowned and focused intently on the flows of earth.

Eilidh couldn't keep her mind on their early scouting of the island. She kept thinking back to their conversation the previous night. Returning to the kingdom, even if she were severed, would extend her life by a thousand years. She hadn't considered that possibility during the past decades. She'd been taught that, as an exile unable to return to the Halls of Mists and walk the magical plane of the Otherworld, she would age faster, although nowhere near as fast as a human. That seemed a blessing to her, condemned and alone as she was. But if she had Imire and Saor beside her, and possibly some of her other friends, if she could once again breathe the kingdom air, would that be worth it? What would she lose? Her earth magic was weak anyway, and she'd never been trained in astral magic. She watched Saor. Perhaps if she wanted to accept his proposal, she shouldn't go any further. What if she was strong in the Path of the Azure? Wouldn't that make it harder to give it up?

"Do you hear something?" he asked.

"No." She opened her mouth to tell him what she'd been thinking but changed her mind. She shook her head and added, "Nothing." Then she noticed a deadness in the air. "They're here."

Saor gave her his full attention, but didn't ask how she knew.

"Don't you feel it?" Eilidh asked.

"Feel what? I feel nothing."

"Exactly," she said. "The kingdom magic is completely disturbed here, as though we were standing in the centre of a human city. The few thousand people around this island would not be able to achieve that on their own."

Saor looked around and she saw his expression change to one of understanding. They stood in a deep forest on an island in the middle of nowhere. A place like this was where the kingdom was usually the strongest. But instead, its influence was minimal. "This isn't right," Saor said. "I've heard there is a gateway nearby."

"If there were, we would be able to smell the Halls of Mist."

Saor didn't argue, but he grew even more tense. The pair continued walking, up the peninsula toward the centre of the island. It took several hours, because they moved with caution in the unfamiliar territory. Suddenly, Saor stopped. "Eilidh," he said and turned to her.

She waited for him to finish, but he said nothing more. "Saor?"

"It's gone," he said. His golden skin turned sallow.

"What's gone?"

"The flows. I can't see the flows."

Eilidh's ability with the Ways had always been so weak she hadn't noticed the change. For her to see the flows, she had to try. For Saor, it was as natural as breathing. Eilidh turned to a nearby tree and whispered, but it did not acknowledge her words. She turned a puzzled expression to Saor. "Speak to the earth. Try."

She'd never seen him so tentative, as though he feared even to say the words. Saor knelt on the hillside and put his hand on a flat, grey stone. Frustration marred his smooth features. In the ancient fae tongue he said, "Water." His forehead wrinkled into a frown. "Path. Strength. Ages." Each word became progressively angrier until he shouted, "Fire!" None of his words had any effect. Stone magic was opposite on the spectrum from her weak air magic, so Eilidh had never been attuned to his casting. But as he spoke the words, she felt their hollowness. Something in this place robbed him of his connection to the earth.

The failure visibly shook Saor. For the first time, she had to acknowledge she hadn't been entirely confident in their mission. Just because Imire heard a few rumours about elder outcasts did not make it so. Still, as she looked around this place and felt the lack of kingdom influence, she grew excited at the idea of meeting another azuri fae. It had been easy to think about giving up talents that had never been anything but a curse to her. But if she were not alone, what would that mean?

She gave Saor's arm a reassuring squeeze and took the lead. Now she dismissed her earlier idea of turning back. She had to do this. It was possible the lack of kingdom influence could be caused by something other than the Path of the Azure. She had no idea what it could be, though, and she was determined to unravel the mystery.

She led Saor, who with each passing hour seemed more troubled. His golden eyes were vacant and fixed on something in the distance. Several times he didn't follow, and she had to double back. She found him heading the way they'd come. "Stay with me," she said softly.

Eilidh led them in a broad curve over the high mountains and past the sheer cliffs. The terrain was rugged, and it slowed them down, but she believed the fae would stay away from people. Wouldn't they? She paused to consider. She didn't stay away from people, so why was she assuming these faeries would? She'd made the same mistake any kingdom fae would make, thinking that human settlements were the antithesis of their power.

With that realisation, she changed direction, heading straight north. She based her judgment on the deadness of the air and how disoriented Saor became. The more agitated he grew, the more confident she was about their direction. To make progress more certain, she began to follow a human road. Few cars passed, with only an occasional bus. Now she held Saor's hand. He had stopped responding to her completely, but at least she did not have to fight him to get him to follow.

Once, Saor stood motionless. Eilidh waited patiently, thinking he might simply need to relieve himself. But instead of saying a word to her, he began to speak with someone, or something, she could not see. He looked down, as though the person was quite small. He turned to Eilidh and said, "We need to go south."

"Why?"

He nodded again in the same downward direction and repeated Eilidh's question. He listened for a moment and said, "She says we'll find the ones we're seeking there."

"No," Eilidh said. "We go north. Come, Saor."

"But..."

"No." It had to be an illusion. Someone wanted to lead them astray. That could only mean whoever cast it must be close. Only an astral faerie could cast illusions, that much she knew. She felt both triumphant and excited, until Saor started to yell.

He jumped and slapped at his arms and legs, as though something crawled all over him.

"Stop." Eilidh put her hands on either side of his face, holding him firmly until he stared into her eyes. "It isn't real, Saor. Trust me." She didn't even want to know what he could have seen to put him in such a state.

"Please, Eilidh," he pled with her. He started to run, but she grabbed him by the arms. They struggled as she forced him to meet her eyes.

"Clear your mind, Saor." She wasn't sure which of her words had the effect, but suddenly Saor calmed. He looked down at his body, then back at her. The panic had gone, but some horror remained. She understood his reaction and why all fae were afraid of illusions. If someone could interfere with the thoughts of even a disciplined faerie like Saor, how could they trust *anything* they saw?

Holding Saor's hand, as much to make sure he didn't wander off as to comfort him, she spoke to the air in a firm, clear voice. "The blessings of the Mother upon you, elder." The forest had an unaccustomed stillness, but she received no reply. "You have severed our connection to the earth. We are no threat to you. We wish only to speak with you."

A soft blue glow appeared on a path ahead. It led away from the road and into the forest. Eilidh approached, leading Saor by the hand, and stopped a few feet away from the glow. It hovered just above a delicate footprint. She examined the mark in the dirt. It appeared to be natural, but Eilidh knew she shouldn't trust her eyes. The glow could be attempting to lead her astray, just as something had done with Saor.

Eilidh stopped and considered. She could take the chance and follow, knowing it might lead them into danger. On the other hand, the footprint pointed further north, not south, as Saor's illusion had. In the end, she could think of no good alternative. As long as she was following an illusion, the caster had to be nearby.

They stepped forward again, and as soon as they reached the glow, it disappeared, but the footprint remained. Just ahead, she caught sight of another blue glow. She went to it and saw the faintest trace of a footprint on the ground again. If Saor had been his normal self, he could have followed the trail unaided. Just as Eilidh had that thought, the glow appeared in front of her. She stepped forward, and it moved a few feet away. The influence no longer showed her footprints, but slowly led her deeper into the woods and over a stream.

After a half hour of walking, they came to a clearing. In the middle was the last thing Eilidh expected to see: a slightly rundown human cottage with a car parked alongside the stone driveway. Sprigs of grass grew around the vehicle, and a small pair of feline eyes peered from underneath it.

The front door opened, and a human woman came out. Her skin had a pinkish glow with freckles across her nose. Hair the colour of rust gathered loosely around her shoulders. She wore jeans and a cropped t-shirt with the word *sugarbabe* across the bosom.

"This is private property," the woman said.

Eilidh opened her mouth to say something, but nothing came out. Why would the strange glow have led her here? Then Eilidh realised what was peculiar about the woman. She stood perfectly still. She waited with the patience a human could never show. "You are fae," Eilidh said.

The woman tilted her head.

A noise came from behind Eilidh, and she turned and saw another woman standing behind her. She had the same colouring as the woman by the house, but she had more angular features. Her expression was also less friendly. "Might as well go up," she said, "since you can't be persuaded to go home."

Everything about her said, *You aren't welcome here*, but Eilidh had a job to do, so she led Saor onward.

∞

The three other druids—Douglas, Rory and Phil— all had talents with the element of water. They were friendly enough, but they acted wary and showed consistency in their disbelief that Munro's abilities had spontaneously emerged. Although Munro was now fairly sure Eilidh had uncovered his abilities, he had to stick with his story. They also insisted on a demonstration of his powers before they would speak openly, even though Frankie told him they were cousins.

"I'm not sure I can do anything on command," he said. "It always happens when I'm not thinking about it." They were sitting around a white, metal table in Rory's back garden. The sky had taken on the flat, pale grey it did on late summer nights, when the sun stayed up until nearly midnight. He showed them the bear and the teardrop he'd made and explained how it happened.

Douglas and Phil seemed satisfied, but not Rory. "Stone, you say? That's pretty rare."

"Is it?" Munro shrugged. "Just seems like rocks and metal are the only thing that have done anything for me. I don't really know all that much about it."

Rory picked up the stone teardrop and held it by the wide, bulbous end. A green glow so faint Munro thought it might be a trick of the light emanated from Rory's fingertips. A single drop of water slid down the channel to the tear's point and splattered onto the table. "It's a genuine piece," he said finally.

Frankie explained, "All druids use talismans like those, although some of us are better than others at making them. The medium tends to depend on the talent. Since the four of us are attuned with water, wood works best for us." He started to go on, but Rory cut him off.

Rory tapped the teardrop onto the top of the metal bear's head. "What we don't know is who made them." He seemed to be the leader, with Phil and Douglas staying quiet and taking their cues from him.

"Come on, Rory," Frankie said. "I couldn't have made that. Could you? There aren't any other stone druids around. Only someone with talent in stone or fire could have made that."

Rory reluctantly handed the piece back. "You're a copper, right?"

Munro nodded. Frankie had told them about his job when they'd all been introduced.

"So you probably saw Craig Laughlin then."

Munro froze. Craig Laughlin was the second victim, the one whose heart exploded. "No," he said. "I never saw him. I'd been off sick and wasn't working that night. You knew him?"

Douglas sat forward. "What kind of sick?"

Munro didn't want to talk about it. "Passed out at work. Had a seizure or something. It's all bogus. The docs can't find anything wrong. Probably was just stress." He shrugged.

Douglas and Phil exchanged a look, and Rory relented. "Sounds like what happened to most of us. Unlocking isn't an easy process. That's why we're surprised it happened on its own. I've never heard of that."

"What does this have to do with Craig Laughlin?" Munro asked.

Frankie leaned over and said quietly, "He was one of us."

"A stone druid like you," Douglas added.

Rory cast a glare that silenced the entire table.

Just then, the side gate opened and two more men walked through. One was tall and lanky in a black t-shirt and ripped jeans, while the other had an athlete's build and buzzed blond hair. "Hey," the tall one said to Rory, then stopped when he saw Munro. He looked him over for a second and turned his attention back to Rory. "Boss wants us," he said.

"Boss?" Munro asked. He had a feeling it wasn't an employer. Not at this time of night.

Frankie chuckled. "That's just what Aaron calls our mentor, Cridhe. We gotta go though. You can take my car back to my house to get yours. I'll get a lift with one of the guys."

Cridhe? It could be a fae name, but then it could be some kind of nickname too. "Your mentor? Can I tag along? Maybe he can help me figure out how my abilities got unlocked."

"Sure," Frankie said. "He'll want to meet you." He glanced at Rory and the new arrivals, but no one raised an objection.

Just then, Munro's mobile rang. He put the phone to his ear. "Munro," he said. He listened and glanced up at the five men. "Christ," he muttered as he hung up. To the group he said, "Sorry, it'll have to be another night. I've got to work." He turned to Frankie. "Does the offer of your car still stand? I have to go in right away."

Frankie frowned. "Another murder? Already?"

The response unsettled Munro, as though his cousin assumed there would be another killing and was only surprised by the timing. Instead of answering, Munro thanked his host and said goodbye to the others. "Nice to meet you all," he said with a wave as he took Frankie's keys.

His cousin followed him out to the car. "The gear box sticks a little," he said, opening the driver's side door.

Munro nodded. "Thanks. I'll put the key through the mail slot." He paused before he climbed in. "Do you know something about these killings I should know?"

Frankie seemed troubled but covered it quickly. "You know how this city is. Everybody knows everybody."

Munro nodded. "Sorry about your friend." He half expected Frankie to make a clichéd comment urging him to stop whoever was committing the crimes, but he didn't say a word.

CHAPTER 14

THE STRANGE-LOOKING FAERIES invited Eilidh and Saor inside. Saor seemed less glassy-eyed than he had been, but he still carried a hollow expression. He naturally felt the loss of the Ways of Earth more keenly than she did. For her it was as though she couldn't smell something others could. For him, she thought, it must feel like total blindness.

If the outside of the house appeared perfectly human, the inside was anything but. One wall was covered in rock with embedded purple crystals that made the light dance around the room. When one of their hosts saw Eilidh's interest she said, "It enhances the resonance." Every piece of furniture was of fae design and hand crafted. The home had a beautiful, flowing elegance that showed the work of an artist. A hand-woven tapestry hung over one wall, blocking out the windows. It depicted a scene from the Halls of Mist that made Eilidh's heart ache with the distant memory.

"I am Beniss," the first woman said. Although her body appeared human, when Eilidh got a close look, she knew Beniss couldn't be anything but fae. Her hair shone like polished copper, and her eyes had an inner gleam. "And this is Galen."

Eilidh introduced herself and Saor, and they both bowed formally to their host.

Galen gave the slightest bow in response, but said nothing. Instead, she raised an eyebrow to Beniss, who acknowledged it with a nod. Galen left without another word.

"You must forgive my sister," Beniss said. "She is distrustful of kingdom fae." Her gaze settled pointedly on Saor and she remarked, "You still have the scent of the Otherworld on you." With a glance at Eilidh she said, "But you...you have been away from the kingdom for some time." She laughed suddenly. "I have forgotten my manners. It has been so long since an outsider has come here that I hardly remember how to behave. Would you like some honeyed froth?"

They accepted with gratitude. The long journey had tired them both. Beniss left them in the living area where they sat on the low, inclined seats their people favoured. Eilidh felt more comfortable than she had in a long time. She only wished Saor felt at ease.

When Beniss returned, Eilidh asked, "Why have you severed the earth flows?"

Beniss smiled sadly and gave them each a cup of a warm, sweet beverage. "You must think us rude, but over the centuries we have learned to be cautious.

Of course, I would alleviate his discomfort if I could, but the enchantment is one that covers a wide area, lasts a very long time, and is difficult to produce. If Saor does not wish to stay, Galen would gladly escort him off the island."

Eilidh found it interesting that Beniss only addressed herself to Eilidh, never directly to Saor. Eilidh turned a questioning glance to Saor.

"No," Saor said, also speaking only to Eilidh. "I won't leave you." His voice was strained and tired.

Beniss nodded at his decision and then said, "I would ask what brings you to Skye, but I can guess. You obviously are weak in the Ways of Earth, or you would feel as disoriented as your friend. Since no faerie would voluntarily stay away from the Otherworld as long as you obviously have, I have to assume you are...an exile?"

Eilidh tilted her head. She found Beniss so strange. She appeared to be a human teenager, with her freckles and round ears, spoke like a fae elder, but felt like neither. "I'll start at the beginning, if that's all right?" Eilidh said.

"Please." Beniss crossed her legs in her chair, gesturing for Eilidh to continue. "We still keep to the night."

Eilidh began slowly, finding it painful to recount her childhood fumbling with the Ways of Earth and how awkward she'd felt. Beniss waited with immaculate patience for Eilidh to continue. When it came time for Eilidh to reveal how she had discovered the illusion spells and the mindspeaking talents, she picked up the pace. She let loose the anger and frustration she'd experienced when her father tried to keep her from casting in certain ways, always returning her to the Ways of Earth, making her repeat uncooperative incantations over and over.

If he thought he could drive her affinity with the Path of the Azure away by sheer stubborn will, Eilidh proved him wrong. She tried to be dutiful, accepting his explanation that certain spells and talents were forbidden, but small things kept popping up. She had an exceptional memory and could recount an event with the exact inflection of every speaker. Once, she found she could change someone's mind with a suggestion. It was a small thing. An instructor gave her an afternoon off when he intended to keep her working long into the night.

Her father, unfortunately, soon learned what she'd done. He punished her severely, but did not make her go back to the instructor. Imire told her she must never, ever influence another faerie's mind again. He wove a story of the horrible consequences of robbing others of their free will. It made a lasting impression on her, and she never tried again, not even when her freedom was at stake.

Saor turned his face away when she talked about her isolation, the death sentence, and finally her father's plan for her escape.

Beniss watched them both carefully. When Eilidh went silent she said, "And since leaving the kingdom? Have you discovered more of your talents?"

Eilidh shook her head. "I do not cast the azure," she said.

Beniss narrowed her eyes in disapproval. "An entire youth wasted. Well, we can only work with what we have." She looked from Eilidh to Saor and back. "You are tired. You've come a long way. I think you should rest now. The night is only half over, but I suspect you will sleep through the day. But tomorrow night is soon enough to sort out where you will live and when your training will begin." With a nod to Saor she added, "I'm not sure how the others will feel about him staying amongst us, but we can talk about that tomorrow."

Eilidh stopped her. "You misunderstand. It's not for myself that I am here."

Beniss raised a slim auburn eyebrow. "No?"

"There is another who can cast the Path of the Azure. I do not know him, but he brings death with him. He has murdered at least two already." Eilidh pushed through her weariness and told Beniss about the faerie who killed with blood shadows, how the kingdom conclave refused to help.

They sat in silence for a time after Eilidh finished her story. Beniss frowned and appeared to weigh Eilidh's words carefully. Finally, Beniss said, "I will speak to the High Conclave. You must go rest now. I insist. You look as though you would fall over." When Eilidh began to protest Beniss said, "I promise I will speak well for you. I do not know what, if anything, we can do, but your news troubles me."

Eilidh's heart sank. Another conclave that likely would do nothing. Had she wasted days on this journey for naught? She was too tired to protest. "Thank you, Beniss. You are kind to accept two strangers into your home."

Beniss smiled. "I hope you will be comfortable." She stood and showed Eilidh and Saor to a room in the back of the cottage. It contained a wide swing bed suspended from a wooden frame. Even the blankets were hand-woven.

It made Eilidh homesick all over again. "Thank you," she said.

"You are welcome here," Beniss replied and left them alone to sleep.

∞

The village of Comrie fell under Tayside Police's Western Division. Minor crimes there would usually be handled by beat officers out of the Crieff station. However, the link to the Perth murders meant the Dewer task force got the call. In his role as POLSA, police search advisor, Sergeant Hallward called specialist searchers to the scene. Munro was grateful he'd taken on the extra training required to become part of that group. Otherwise, he never would have gotten near the scene, and once again, all his information would have come second-hand.

Although it was after 9:00 p.m. when Munro arrived, the hazy summer light meant they would search the area that night. He passed the village, drove on to a place called the Twenty Shilling Woods, and stopped when he saw the line of police cars.

He and another thirty officers were organised in a grid over the uneven ground surrounding a mound in the middle of a field. On the top of the mound were four standing stones. In the centre of the stones, CID had erected a crime scene tent to protect the body from the elements. The body had been removed, of course, before the searchers could assemble for their part of the process, but Munro didn't need to see the corpse to learn what had happened.

Munro was suddenly overwhelmed by a feeling of helplessness. He had information about the crime. Although he didn't know the killer's name and address, he knew who it was. Now he understood that his cousin Frankie and the other druids had information about the crimes. He knew he should tell Sergeant Hallward, but what evidence did he have that the druids were involved? None. All Munro had was suspicion, based on the fact that they knew the second victim and that Craig Laughlin had been a druid. A lot of people had probably known the guy. As Frankie said, everybody knew everybody in a place like Perth.

"Waiting for an engraved invitation, PC Munro?" Hallward's voice boomed through the eerie summer night.

"No, Sarge." Munro took his place at the edge of the search grid and began the long, tedious process of combing through every blade of grass in the field.

The search was pointless. This whole sham of procedure rankled him, but he needed to find out what he could about the crime so he could tell Eilidh.

Eilidh. He wondered where she was and if he'd ever see her again. He no longer felt the connection to her, and he couldn't even feel the faint flicker of her presence. She'd said she was going to get help, and he had believed her. On the other hand, she'd also said she couldn't face the blood faerie alone. If she couldn't, he doubted *his* help was going to push her over the top of the power scale. He also didn't dare hope she was coming back with the cavalry. What if she hadn't even made it? It was a few hundred miles to Skye and back, and Eilidh and Saor were going to bloody run there.

Munro shook his head and kept up the appearance of a careful search, all the while trying to convince himself that he wanted Eilidh back to stop the killings and not for personal, selfish reasons. Not because he wanted to sit and talk with her for hours, to find out every little thing about her. Not because he wanted nothing more than to show her every human invention, to teach her about his world and learn about hers. Not because she was mesmerizingly beautiful.

By midnight, it was getting dark, so Hallward called off the search. The sun would make its reappearance around four the next morning, and Hallward wanted everyone back by five. As Munro walked across the already-searched field toward his car, he saw the faintest of glows. If he hadn't been right on top of it, he never would have seen it. He walked over casually and crouched down to brush the grass aside. Nestled in the dirt, a flat, circular stone about the size of Munro's palm lay half buried.

It didn't look like anything special, so Munro wasn't surprised the searcher who'd covered this area hadn't given it a second glance. Munro tugged the stone out of the loose ground, and flipped it over in his hand. One side was perfectly smooth, but the other bore intricate carvings with swirls and runes. An image of a burning sun covered the centre. It flashed briefly in his hand, and Munro nearly dropped the disk in surprise.

"Munro, what the hell are you doing? If you find something, you aren't supposed to touch it." Hallward strode across the grass toward Munro.

Munro stood and turned the rock to show the flat side. "It's nothing, Sarge. Just a rock." He shrugged and tried to look sheepish, holding the stone up for Hallward to see.

The sergeant seemed mollified, but he continued to walk toward Munro and examined the rock up close. Fortunately, he didn't take it or turn it over.

"Same as the others?" Munro said, gesturing toward the low mound where the body had been discovered.

"Seems like it."

Something in his tone made Munro ask, "What's different?"

"Two victims."

"Two?" Munro didn't know what to think about that.

"Definitely our killer. One heart missing, one heart removed but destroyed. They've been out here a while, at least a week before Dewer. The second body had his throat cut." Hallward nodded toward the white tent. "Doc says he must have had some kind of genetic disorder. Or maybe extensive plastic surgery. We'll know more after the autopsy." He paused for a moment, then added, "You'd better get going, Munro. We have a long day ahead of us tomorrow. Get some sleep while you can. This bastard isn't going anywhere."

Munro's chest tightened. *Genetic disorder or plastic surgery?* Something had looked odd about the body then. Munro knew in his gut the second victim was fae. *Hurry, Eilidh.*

CHAPTER 15

WHEN EILIDH AWOKE LATE the next day, she found herself tangled in Saor's arms, rocking softly in the suspended fae bed. He lay beside her, watching her. It felt so comfortable and familiar that Eilidh was tempted to stay there for hours. She smiled and stretched, extricating herself from his embrace. She had enjoyed the moment, but soon reality came crashing back. This wasn't the old days, she wasn't a kingdom fae, and Saor was no longer hers.

"I've missed you," Saor said and paused. "I know you're angry with me because I didn't visit you."

Eilidh squeezed his hand. "I'm not angry. I was confused for a time, but it soon became clear to me that you did the right thing. If you'd followed your heart and come to me, no good would come of it."

"None?"

Part of Eilidh would have liked to condemn him for the choices he'd made decades ago, but it wouldn't be fair. Although he hadn't done what she would have, he'd made the right choice. Being tainted with her crimes would have done neither of them any good.

"Have you thought about what we discussed before?"

Of course she had. She found it difficult to think about much else. But last night, as Eilidh told their host about the blood faerie, the real dangers to so many people became clear in her mind. She realised that no matter what she may want for herself, she was unwilling to abandon the cause she and Munro had set out to tackle together. While most kingdom fae might not care about a few human deaths, she could no longer pretend they didn't matter.

Rather than answer the question, Eilidh changed the subject. "You seem to be feeling better. Can you feel the source?"

"No. It feels as though colour has gone out of the world. But I think the night's rest has done me good." Saor reached for Eilidh, but she stirred and began to straighten her clothes.

"Eilidh, you didn't answer my question."

"Saor—"

"I don't blame you. You were born this way. I understand that. Especially after hearing you speak last night. I never appreciated the things you went through. I thought I knew you well, but perhaps that was my mistake. I didn't understand how much you were holding back, hoping to protect me." Saor watched Eilidh, his golden eyes swirling with emotion.

"Saor, I don't think there's any going back for me."

"You would give up without even trying?"

"First we should hear what Beniss has to say. I don't hold out much hope. It sounds like this so-called higher conclave could be a lot like the kingdom conclave. After all, fae is fae. It was foolish of me to think they would behave differently. It must be in the blood." Eilidh smiled sadly.

Saor began to respond, but stopped when they heard footfalls coming toward their room. Beniss appeared, looking weary, as though while Eilidh and Saor slept, she found no rest at all. "Come," she said. "The conclave wishes to meet you."

"Beniss," Eilidh began. "If you don't mind me asking, why do you look human?"

"Can't you guess?" Beniss' green eyes sparkled with amusement.

It was Saor who answered. "Illusion." He seemed distinctly uncomfortable.

"Yes. And I will admit, it appeals to my sense of humour." She shrugged. "We protect our little community. We live close to the human settlements, and it's much easier to blend in if we can pass for them." Beniss led them into the kitchen where she served a simple meal of fruit, bread, and honey. She seemed distracted and impatient, but she didn't offer further comment.

"How many of you live here?" Saor asked after a few moments of silence. "We were told three, but if there are enough of you to form a conclave, I would suppose we have been misinformed."

Beniss smiled. "That was true, at one time. Over the years, two more joined us. And we have been blessed."

Eilidh was aware that Beniss, her sister, and the third faerie exiled with them had been banished from the kingdom nearly a thousand years before. In that time, she supposed, it was feasible they'd produced one or two children per couple, and those children *might* have had children, but that could hardly be called a conclave, which traditionally needed at least twelve. There was little point in having a conclave of twelve to rule twelve, but any birth among the fae was something to be celebrated. "That's wonderful," she said. "Are your children gifted in the same way you are?"

It was something she'd wondered once upon a time, but she hadn't contemplated it for a while. But in considering Saor's wish for her to once again be a part of the kingdom, she thought about what it might mean to give birth to a faerie cursed with forbidden magic. But neither her parents nor grandparents had shown any signs of being afflicted by the Path of the Azure, so perhaps it was not inevitable.

"Although the chance of azuri talents is much greater among our children, the Mother of the Earth and the Father of the Azure choose our strengths," Beniss explained. "Our children who are gifted in the Path stay with us out of necessity. The others moved on. They could not be expected to remain where their gifts in the Ways of Earth could not manifest.

"We have a few allies living among the kingdom who help us by taking in the children who need guidance in the Ways of Earth. After all, what faerie would not welcome a child in these days of dwindling numbers?" She saw that Eilidh and Saor had finished eating. "Come, you will meet the others." She guided them outside, and they followed her down a path behind the small house. They walked for some time in silence, and Eilidh grew more agitated and nervous. Although the conclave would, she hoped, be kinder to her than the last one she faced, unwanted memories and feelings surfaced.

Instead of going further into the woods, Beniss led them to a paved road, and they walked for several miles, coming close to a human village. Eilidh retrieved her small black hat from her pocket and covered her ears, and Saor lifted his hood.

Eilidh expected to pass through the village or perhaps turn down a forgotten byway. Instead, they walked directly to a building marked *Village Hall* and entered. That was not the most surprising thing. The hall was full of what appeared at first glance to be humans. It didn't take long for Eilidh to see that the human faces were an illusory facade. A moment later, her ears picked up the delicate sound of the ancient fae tongue. The voices speaking it had a pure, clear tone that could not be human.

There were faeries of many ages, including a few small children who ran around the hall playing. But their appearance wasn't what shocked her. What surprised her was their number. She counted at least forty in the room. In a thousand years, a fae couple might be blessed with one or two births, if any. But forty? Beniss had said that some of the children had chosen not to stay with them. Never in her life could she have imagined this was possible.

The sounds in the hall hushed. All but the children stopped and watched the newcomers. When the faeries saw Beniss, they relaxed. Most went back to what they were doing before Eilidh and Saor had arrived.

Beniss motioned for the pair to follow her. She led them through the hall toward a back corridor. They left the bustling sounds behind and entered a small side room. Inside sat Galen and an elder fae. The elder, unlike the others, did not hide behind an illusion of humanity. Long white hair hung loose around his shoulders, and his face bore deep lines around his eyes and mouth, something that would take more than a thousand years for a kingdom fae. He smiled and waved the new arrivals inside.

"Eilidh, Saor," Beniss said. "Let me introduce you to the head of our conclave, Oron."

Eilidh was not surprised to learn that Oron held that position, one that traditionally went to the most powerful in a community, who was also often the eldest; however, she was surprised to see just how old he was. It was possible, she supposed, that the age on his face was an illusion, just as the youth and humanity on Beniss' face. On the other hand, she couldn't imagine a faerie with any self-respect doing such a thing.

"Sit," Oron said, pointing at some chairs along the back wall. The trio each grabbed a chair and sat as he'd requested. "I thought it might be a little easier to meet with me one-on-one," he said. "From what Beniss has told me, it doesn't sound like your previous encounter with a conclave was pleasant. Although it's been a while, I grant you that I certainly remember the feeling." Although his expression was open and friendly, all that changed when he turned his eyes on Saor. "You, kingdom faerie, have been allowed into our community on Beniss' word that you have come here in good faith and that you are bound by friendship to one who follows the Path. However, take me at my word, if you ever betray us, our community, our location, our numbers, our strengths and weaknesses, I will learn of it, and you *will* regret it. Understood?"

There was no mistaking the menace in Oron's voice. Eilidh had no doubt he could and would find a way to make Saor regret any word spoken in the wrong ear. An elder of the kingdom would be a dangerous enemy. She didn't even want to think what an elder of the Path of the Azure could do. Apparently, Saor also understood and believed Oron's warning, because he inclined his head and replied, "Indeed."

As quickly as it had come upon him, with Saor's agreement, the serious expression left Oron's face. He once again appeared welcoming and jovial. He asked Eilidh to repeat the story she'd told Beniss the night they arrived, and Eilidh did as he requested. This time the telling was briefer and less emotional, simply because she'd told it before.

"You are welcome among us, Eilidh. I suspect you have many questions and much to learn about the Path of the Azure. Believe me, what you learned from the kingdom conclave is not the truth, or at least not the *whole* truth. But Beniss tells me you have other things on your mind. This news concerns us as well. I have heard of the type of magic the blood faerie wields, and once, long ago, I even saw it practiced." He paused as though remembering something. "Did you know there was a time when the Path of the Azure was called higher magic, and those who had the talent for it were revered among all faeries?" He didn't wait for her to answer. "Yes, once we held positions of power in the kingdom, until a few misguided souls allowed their greed to corrupt them. They were not satisfied with simply wielding the magic of the azure. Wicked fools."

"What happened?" Eilidh asked.

"They taught you, I suppose, that using the magic of the Path of the Azure is corrupting, addictive, and perhaps even evil?" Again, Oron didn't wait for an answer. "It is not the flows themselves that cause the hearts of the fae to become corrupt, any more than the Ways of Earth could cause such malignancy." Saor opened his mouth to interrupt Oron, but the elder ignored him. "It is the power itself. Consider this. Why do you believe, Eilidh, the kingdom conclave ordered your death?"

"Because I know forbidden magic." Eilidh didn't understand what Oron was asking.

"But why is it forbidden?"

She thought of the obvious answer but knew that wasn't what he wanted. He believed the Path of the Azure was not evil or corrupting as she'd been taught. But if that were not the case, why would the kingdom conclave send out an edict declaring the Path of the Azure forbidden? She looked at Oron and shook her head.

It was Saor who offered the answer. "Because they were afraid."

A smile broke out on Oron's face. "Precisely. With the power of the Path of the Azure, we could have dominated the kingdom and everyone in it. We could have put one of our own on the throne. We might have even challenged the other kingdoms and began a war like our race has not seen in several millennia."

Eilidh shivered. Yes, she could understand why the kingdom fae had been so afraid. Never in her wildest dreams would it have occurred to her to try to depose the royal family. It was unthinkable, even to an outcast like her.

Oron went on. "Our ability is rare outside our own direct descendants, although it certainly does pop up spontaneously now and again. You are proof of that, Eilidh. And as they still seem to do, the kingdom conclave of my youth feared that we of the Path would set up our own royal dynasty. In truth, had we been as organised and ruthless as they suspected us to be, they could not have stopped us.

Our downfall, it seems, was our unwillingness to become what they thought we were."

"And yet," Saor said, "there is one of the Path murdering humans in the most bizarre and indiscriminate manner. If that is not the definition of insanity, I'm not sure how you would categorise it."

"Evil is not the sole provenance of the Path," Oron responded. When Saor agreed, albeit reluctantly, Oron went on to explain. "But I will concede this point. Those that deal in blood have sometimes proved to enjoy the flows in a way I personally find distasteful." Oron appeared thoughtful. "Eilidh, I know you have not chosen to study with us yet, although I hope that someday you will find your home among us, at least for a time. There is much we could teach you, and there is much you could add to our number as well. Even understanding that, I think there are some things you should know about us, about yourself, about the magic that flows through you.

"As there are four spheres of earthbound flows, once there were four spheres of the azuri as well. The Path of the Azure consists of the astral, the flows you and I wield, blood magic, of which I know very little, and two further realms. Spirit flows and temporal flows have been lost to this world. None of us in the higher conclave know why, but there has not been a fae in any kingdom born of the spirit or temporal flows in five thousand years. That is arguably a good thing, for they could manipulate the soul and time itself, two things that are dangerous in the hands of anyone. I certainly would never wish to have such power.

"We who wield the azuri flows get our power from the stars, and our sphere of control is the mind. For blood fae, known in my day also as bone fae, their power comes from within. If their heart becomes corrupted however, they may seek to use the blood and bone of others to achieve their means."

"How do we know what their aim may be?" Eilidh asked.

"Tell me what you know of the deaths," Oron said.

Eilidh described the body as she found it under her church tower, as well as the body she had seen whose heart was removed from the chest cavity, but left damaged at the scene.

Oron's face twisted into an expression of extreme distaste as she recounted the details. "As I said before, I am not well versed in the ways of bone magic. Before we were cast out of the kingdom, there were more of our number, and we displayed varying talents. Sadly, many perished in the rebellion."

Rebellion?

"But I can tell you this much, whatever ritual this blood faerie has begun, he has not finished yet."

Saor interrupted. "How can you be certain?"

"Obviously his last killing did not achieve what he wanted. The heart is the source of a faerie's power, even those of us whose sphere is the mind or the earth. We can train to still our minds, but our hearts beat one measure after another without thought, without intention. For the fae, our magic is in our blood, literally speaking. So to take our blood, or to take the heart that controls the flows within us, is to capture our essence."

"But all of the victims were human," Eilidh said.

"The only time I have ever heard of humans being a part of a fae ritual," Oron said, "was when the human was a true druid. But I haven't seen one of those since my exile. In fact, I don't think any still exist."

Sudden panic clutched at Eilidh's heart. *Munro.* "I have met one," she said in a rush. "He has the ability to mould stone."

Oron became quite excited. "You have bound a true druid to yourself?"

"Bound? My father mentioned this to me but I do not understand."

"If the power of one of the Path is two or three times what an earth faerie might possess, the power of an azuri faerie when combined with that of a true druid is ten times. As you have probably noticed, we are weak in the earth. But a true druid can compensate and give us full control of the Ways of Earth."

"You mean Eilidh could master stone?" Saor asked.

Oron leaned forward. He gazed into Eilidh's eyes. "If you bind this true druid to you, you could master all the Ways, not just stone."

"All the Ways?" Eilidh looked from Oron to Beniss and back again.

"Air, water, stone, fire." Oron nodded. "Like any of the flows, they would take time to master. Ability is one thing; competency is another. But as the magic in your blood increases your lifespan, so will the limited magic in his blood increase his, and the bond you share will add to that even more."

"What would I have to do to bind him, and what would be the cost to him?"

Oron smiled. "A wise question, child. But perhaps we'll talk about that after you have met some of the others and we have discussed this blood ritual further. My bigger concern is the immediate threat. If the blood faerie is killing true druids to perform some dark ritual, this is a grave concern to all of us who follow the Path of the Azure. To lose even one druid is a tragedy. Either this bone faerie does not know what he is doing, or he is sacrificing them for something that will bring him such power that losing a few druids is meaningless. Neither of these possibilities is good."

Beniss stood. "Oron is right. We have talked for a long time. I know your need is pressing, so we must speak to the others. Return to my home, and I will find you after the conclave has met once again."

Although Eilidh did not like having to wait, her mind buzzed with all the things she'd learned. She needed some fresh air and time to sort things out in her mind. Her heart was suddenly full of worry for Munro. If the blood faerie was killing only true druids, then Munro was in danger, and she needed to warn him. It shocked her that she cared so much, after knowing him only a short time. She knew her concern didn't just come from learning that he could enhance her power. She was curious, true. She felt a tingling hope she had never experienced before, that she might not just be some magically malformed aberration to be shunned and hated. But more than that, he was her friend, and perhaps their relationship could grow even further, although she barely let herself think that way. She would never forgive herself if something happened to him that she could have stopped.

∞

Cridhe stared at his human minions. "Are you certain he is gifted with stone?" He glanced from Douglas to Rory and then Phil, finally letting his gaze settle on Frankie, Munro's cousin. "Absolutely certain?"

The three other druids looked at Frankie for confirmation, and he nodded.

Interesting. Cridhe thought he would have to put his plans on hold indefinitely since the disaster with Craig Laughlin. He wasn't sure why the ritual failed, only that it had done so in a spectacular way. He'd taken the heart the same way he'd done with Robert Dewar and as Dudlach had with Jon. But as soon as Cridhe got two feet away from Craig's body, the beating heart, the magically bound organ, began to quiver and shake in Cridhe's hand. The druid's essence had been encapsulated in his heart, but Cridhe could not get it to stay there, and it had burst out of its delicate fleshy cage.

Dudlach had been quite angry at Cridhe's failure. He'd stood over his son, screaming with rage. Cridhe bore the insults with grinding teeth. His father was dead. Why wouldn't he leave him alone?

Cridhe had no choice but to wait until they found another stone druid. The instructions on the slab had been most specific. But even without them, Cridhe could tell by the resonance of the flows that only stone magic would do. Now one had been delivered to them. It couldn't have been more perfect. Finally, Dudlach was silent.

The four druids sitting in front of Cridhe all had talents in the water element, the most common. So he knew he could take any of them at any time. Dudlach wanted him to choose the most powerful of each sphere they could find, thinking it might make a difference to the success of the ritual. But Cridhe didn't think it would matter. Balance was the thing. It would be better to have four druids of equal talent, rather than one or two who outshone the other sacrifices. Without balance, one flow might overpower the others, causing the result to be uneven and therefore less powerful. The last thing they wanted was an unpredictable result of something of this magnitude.

It rankled him still that he'd had to sacrifice Jon, whom he missed every day. They had been the most potent combination, and everything seemed easier for Cridhe when Jon was around. Dudlach said that was nonsense, but Cridhe knew what he felt, and he would not be denied his revenge. He had to tolerate Dudlach for now, but that would not remain true forever. Once he had Eilidh by his side, his first order of business would be to find a way to rid himself of his father's influence, no matter the cost.

Everything they had planned would come together, and all of his dreams would be within his grasp as soon as he had the druid Munro. With his gifts of stone, Munro was destined to be a sacrifice. For the first time, Cridhe contemplated believing in the Great Mother. His father had taught him to respect and fear the Father and Mother, but Cridhe thought them part of the alien kingdom ways. But Cridhe knew those ways enough to see the kingdom had something he wanted, something that would be his very soon, thanks to Munro.

"Master, my cousin said his powers unlocked spontaneously. You told us that was impossible. He claims it happened at the church." Frankie paused, as though not certain he wanted to continue.

"Church?" Cridhe said absentmindedly.

"St Paul's," he said, and then continued when Cridhe did not answer. "Where Robert…"

"Where he what?" Cridhe snapped.

"Well, sir. Munro is a cop. He found Robert's body. Could that have caused his abilities to come out? I mean, I keep wondering exactly how it might have happened."

Cridhe froze. He sat in perfect stillness as though time had stopped, and all the pieces of the puzzle slid into place. *Eilidh*. Was Munro the human he saw with her the night he killed Craig Laughlin? The night *she* chased *him*? How delightful that had been. If he hadn't so distracted by his failure with harvesting Craig Laughlin's heart that night, he would have been tempted to play with her.

"Master?"

Eilidh must have found Munro and nurtured his talents the same way he had nurtured Jon's. Suddenly, everything felt perfect and right. "Bring him to me. I'd like to meet this Munro."

CHAPTER 16

EILIDH AND SAOR HAD BARELY talked since they returned to Beniss' house. Eilidh had too much on her mind. Her thoughts flooded with possibilities she had never allowed herself to even dream about. Saor, on the other hand, stalked around like a man trapped. Finally, when no word had come from the higher conclave for some time, Saor stopped pacing directly in front of Eilidh. He put a hand on her shoulders and peered into her eyes. "It's not too late to put this all behind you," he said. "Nothing has changed."

Eilidh stared at him for a moment, disbelieving. "Everything has changed, Saor. How can you not see that?"

"What would you do? Are you prepared to take the druid, make yourself the most powerful faerie the kingdom has ever seen, and challenge the throne yourself?"

She stepped back from his touch. "How can you say such a thing? Are you truly so blinded by jealousy that you refuse to understand the truth when it's laid out for you? Does it so destroy the image you have of me to think I could be something other than a magical cripple? What claim do you have to be jealous anyway?"

"You were meant for me. You were made for me."

"There was a time I would have given anything to hear you say that."

Saor gave a bitter laugh. "But no longer. You have been infected with humanity."

Eilidh did not answer. She looked at Saor and did not recognise him. He would still ask her to go back to the kingdom and have her talents severed so she could never touch magic again. That realisation was particularly bitter, for since coming to the Isle of Skye, he knew what it felt like to have his connection with the Ways stifled. And now that she was beginning to see what might open up for her in the Path of the Azure, she didn't want to give it up with her eyes closed.

For the first time since she'd found the body beneath the church tower, she felt hope. If she learned how to bind Munro to her, she might stand a chance against the blood faerie that threatened her home. Yes, she realised it now, the human city had become her home. She thought about Munro and wondered what it might be like if she didn't turn him away. She did not know what would happen, but she knew that, unlike Saor, Munro would never ask her to give up herself to please him.

Beniss' voice interrupted from the doorway. "I know this must be difficult for both of you."

Saor said nothing.

Eilidh turned to their host. "What did the conclave say?"

"Come," Beniss said. "Let us sit." She led them into the room where they'd talked the first night. They made themselves comfortable, and Beniss began to speak. "There is a ritual. One of my granddaughters heard of it in her travels." Beniss smiled with pride. "She is a scholarly, intelligent faerie. As far as I know, this ritual has never been successfully performed, but if someone were to unlock the potential within it..." Beniss shuddered and looked away.

Eilidh waited patiently for Beniss to continue. Saor, on the other hand, was uncharacteristically distracted and uninterested.

"It is known in the texts as the Krostach Ritual. We cannot be certain this is the rite the blood faerie wishes to complete. I pray to the Great Mother we're wrong."

"What does the ritual do?" Eilidh asked.

"It is dark, dark magic, and none since its creator have had the talent to cast it successfully. It is surprising that any record of how to fulfil its requirements still exists. Genoa, my granddaughter, found only the most obscure references to it. She is not certain exactly what would be involved, but there is clear reference to harvesting the hearts of four true druids, capturing their essence and with it, their power. When an azuri faerie is bonded with a true druid, the faerie gains access to the Ways of Earth, but would still have to study and learn, as any child would."

"Are you saying the blood faerie is trying to replicate that? If that were so, why would he not simply bond with one of the druids himself?" Eilidh asked.

"Let me finish. First, we're not talking about the power of one druid, but four. Even if all he wanted was to bond with four, although unnatural, that would not be as dire as what he may actually be trying to accomplish. No, it is much worse than that. The Krostach Ritual would enable him to take their very essence within himself. Any blood faerie who took part in this ritual would not only have the capacity for the Ways of Earth, but would gain command of it. The earth would be at his feet. Every spell, every enchantment, every slight manipulation. He would know it all. Even if the faerie were acting alone, the results would be disastrous for any who tried to challenge him."

Saor sat forward and listened for the first time. "The power..."

Eilidh's mind raced as she considered the dreadful possibilities. "There would be no stopping him."

Beniss gave Saor a penetrating stare. "It is an ancient magic requiring a specific source stone. When unlocked, it grants the power to hold and preserve the hearts. It is extremely dangerous to the one trying to control it. Genoa said she read many warnings about the price to the faerie trying to complete the ritual. It would cost him much of his soul, even if it worked perfectly. The slightest misstep could cause a descent into madness. My only guess is that the blood faerie acquired the stone and with it, the instructions for completing the ritual. Even with the price paid, he could challenge the kingdom. With his own blood power enhanced to four times the strength of an azuri faerie bonded with a druid, plus the knowledge and mastery of every earth spell and incantation, who could stand against him? Even a hundred of your warriors could not defeat one so powerful."

Horror dawned on Saor's face. "Powerful and mad. The conclave must be warned."

Eilidh decided not to mention she had tried that already. There had never been much chance they would listen to her. But Saor was right. The ritual must be stopped. "Munro is gifted with stone," Eilidh said. "It is an uncommon gift. He could be in great danger." Munro was not the only human who could be in danger. If kingdom faeries were indifferent to humans, the blood faerie seemed to show even less regard for them than he might an insect buzzing around his head. One so powerful and corrupt would devastate the human population.

"I should hurry for *Munro*?"

Eilidh was shocked at the bitterness in his voice. "The death of any true druid is a tragedy, and bonding with him may be my only hope of stopping the ritual. If he will consent, we may stand a chance. Otherwise, I'm not sure how much I can do."

Saor looked at Beniss. "What of the higher conclave? How far are they willing to go to stop this from happening?"

"We're not without sympathy, but it is not safe for those gifted with the forbidden talents to travel through the kingdom lands, as you well know. Every one of us would forfeit our lives. Until we have some assurance that our children and grandchildren would not be at risk, we will not leave Skye."

Saor's eyes flashed with anger. "If the kingdom falls, do you think you would find a place in the new regime with the blood faerie?"

Beniss ignored his insults and did not answer him.

Eilidh understood, but it pained her that Saor could not. The kingdom rejected her kind, so what loyalty did any who followed the Path of the Azure owe them? It was unlikely the fae here were in any danger from the blood faerie. If she was going to stop this faerie, and she had every intention of doing so, it was not to save the kingdom, their society, or even the Faerie Queen herself. Eilidh would stop him because what he was doing was wrong. He took lives he had no right to, and he threatened those she loved. As she'd said to Imire, evil must be challenged.

Saor snorted at Eilidh. "You too would turn your back on your people?"

How could he be so blind to what they all faced?

"You have forgotten who you are," he said.

"No, Saor. *You*, my friend, have forgotten who I am." Eilidh reached out and placed her hand gently over his. "My gift is in the Path of the Azure. It always has been, from the moment I was born. This is not what I chose, but what I am. You would ask me to give it up, to become less, so you could maintain the fantasy that I am what you had hoped I would be. There was never a reality in that dream."

Saor stirred, and without another word, he went to gather his things from the room they'd shared the night before. He left the house without speaking to Beniss or thanking her for the hospitality. Eilidh understood his pain and silently spoke a prayer to the Great Mother for his safety. She hoped he would reach the conclave quickly and that they would listen to reason. But in her heart, she did not hold much hope.

To Beniss she said, "You will not aid me in my quest to stop this ritual? What of the deaths of the druids? Do you not at least have an interest in seeing those tragedies ended?"

"As I have said, I will not have my family cross into kingdom lands as long as it would mean their deaths. A group of us, even a small one, moving through the forests could be seen as an invading army. The kingdom fae watch our borders closely." She smiled sadly. "You crossed well and safely, but you were fortunate, and you had your earth Watcher to guide you. Others of our kind have not been so lucky. Even the death of a druid will not cause me to risk my children and grandchildren. What small security we have has cost us dearly. I would not have you face this thing alone and unprepared, however, so I will come with you myself."

Relief spread over Eilidh.

"I cannot teach you everything you need to know, but I can give you a small chance. I wish you had come here decades ago. Even a year or a month would have made an enormous difference. I will try, but I cannot guarantee you will be prepared for what we are about to face, or that we two even stand a chance. There is some good news though."

"I would like to hear some good news," Eilidh said with a wry smile.

"You have thought all your life that you are weak, but I can assure you this is not the case. You're strong, Eilidh. Stronger than most of our kind I have seen, both in your gifts and in your character. With time, and practice, and your stubborn determination, you will be strong enough to challenge anyone."

"If only we had time."

"Time I cannot provide. But what small benefit my years of experience can give you, I gladly offer." Beniss put her hand to her freckled human face. Slowly the sun-dotted skin paled and became nearly translucent. Deep wrinkles slid into her face, and her rounded ears began to curl and spiral. It took only seconds for the illusion to disappear, but the effects were striking. Beniss had to be at least as ancient as Oron.

Although Eilidh didn't like to admit it, she felt an awe and respect that must've shown on her face, because Beniss responded with a laugh. "The first thing you should learn, my dear, is not to put so much trust in what you see. I will teach you to reliably cast an illusion, and then I will teach you to dispel one. Our gifts lie with the mind, and there is much more the mind can do than perhaps you realise. But most important, I will help you bind the true druid to yourself. As soon as you do that, all those decades of lessons in the Ways of Earth will bear fruit. We should start now. You have a long and dangerous journey ahead. And without your protection, your druid could be in great danger. He must survive."

∞

In the days that passed since he'd met with Frankie and the other druids, Munro didn't have much time to himself. Frankie invited him more than once to meet his mentor, Cridhe, to learn about his new-found power. But nearly every person in the Tayside Police was working overtime these days, and Munro was no exception. The national media had gotten hold of the story, and some of the more sensational details had leaked out. The DI in charge of the case, Boyle, was apoplectic. He vowed to keep them all so busy that no one would have time to think, much less talk to a reporter. He'd been true to his word, and police visibility was at an all-time high.

In addition to searches, interviewing, and re-interviewing witnesses, part of the job became crowd control. Media outlets from all over set up at various points, including the crime scenes, and that drew even more crowds. The small city of Perth, Scotland had turned into a media hive.

Munro wouldn't have expected to have a moment to think about Eilidh, but he hardly thought about anything else. She had been gone a full week. Although he wanted to trust her, he had a sinking feeling she might not come back. To be fair, why should she? That other faerie, Saor, certainly didn't seem to give a toss about the deaths of a few lowly humans. Munro got the impression Saor's attitude was usual for their kind. He contemplated Saor, who seemed to think he had a claim on Eilidh, and whether he'd been an idiot to let Eilidh go off to the Isle of Skye alone with him. It wasn't the best time to ask for leave, but with his recent medical issues, it wouldn't have been a stretch. Plus, Munro knew the police efforts weren't going to achieve anything. No amount of overtime would lead them to a faerie killing druids. All the hard graft and boots on the ground amounted to pointless hours that stretched an already taxed police force.

Munro was thinking this through as he came to the end of another double shift. Without warning, he felt a familiar tug. *Eilidh*. If the intensity of the sensation was anything to go by, she was coming back and moving quickly. He had no way of knowing how long she would take, but it made his heart lighter to know he would see her soon.

The rest of his boring, tedious day went much slower because of the anticipation, but the relief made it bearable. He had to admit he'd been afraid the kingdom fae had found her. If that had happened, she might not have been *able* to return, even if she wanted to.

As he was about to leave for home, his mobile rang. It was Frankie, once again inviting him out. "You sure have been a hard man to get a hold of lately, Eastwood."

"Aye. You wouldn't believe everything that's been going on at work because of these murders."

"I would. Me and the others are getting nervous, you know." Frankie's tone sounded strained and worried.

"Has something happened?" Frankie had not admitted to Munro that all three of the victims had been druids, and one more had been fae. Over the past couple of days, Munro had only been able to talk to his cousin on the phone. Even in those conversations, Frankie hadn't changed his story or given up any helpful information. Of course, the task force hadn't discovered the connection between the four victims. Knowing didn't make it easier for Munro, who worried his cousin might be next.

"Not exactly. I don't really want to talk about this on the phone. I'm at work. Can we meet up later? I think I might have some idea of what's going on."

"Sure." *Bingo.* "When do you get off?"

"Nine. Come see me around ten?"

"I'll be there." They said goodbye, and a sense of uneasiness settled over Munro. Frankie was scared of something, and Munro didn't know if he could protect him. Maybe if they worked together. He didn't know how strong a blood faerie would be. Hell, he didn't even know what *Eilidh* could do beyond drying her own hair. But he had seen those druids with their hearts ripped out. Anyone who could do something like that, whether faerie or human, was not to be taken lightly. His eyes drifted to the north and he silently wished Eilidh would hurry.

CHAPTER 17

EILIDH CLENCHED HER FISTS on her lap. She did not know how Beniss had talked her into this. Riding in this machine was slower than running. This thing—this bus—rocked and screeched and growled. But Beniss insisted, claiming it would be safer and allow them time to talk. Beniss was concerned about encountering kingdom faeries, pointing out that kingdom fae would not go anywhere near a human vehicle.

During the journey, few humans joined them on the bus. One or two got on in one town and off in another, but for the most part, they were not disturbed. Yet the uncomfortable sensations made it difficult for Eilidh to concentrate on what Beniss was saying. Over the years, Eilidh wondered what it would be like to be in one of these motorised machines. But she never thought she would actually do it, and certainly not at the request of another faerie.

Despite her vague sense of motion sickness, Eilidh felt an underlying emotional calm. In the previous two days, she had come to understand more about magic than she had in her entire life of trying unsuccessfully to learn the Ways of Earth. Throughout her childhood, her father and other mentors attempted to teach her something alien to the way her mind naturally worked. Now that she had her first taste of what astral magic should feel like, she gained confidence. Beneath it twinged a layer of regret for all the wasted years, frustration, and deeply ingrained belief that she was somehow less than the other kingdom fae.

Eilidh caught her own reflection in the bus window. The general shape of her face was her own, but Beniss had guided her through creating an illusion to round her ears, darken the shade of her hair and finely arched brows, and add a few flaws to her skin tone. It hardly took any energy for Eilidh to hold the illusion, but it still felt uncomfortable, like wearing a pair of shoes the wrong size. She couldn't help but stare at herself, and she ran her hand over the top of her ears to be sure the spirals were still there, hidden beneath the illusion. Beniss told her that one day she would teach her how to perform an illusion that would fool the mind on a deeper level and make the ears feel as well as look round. For now, however, all they cared about was getting back to Perth without being noticed.

Eilidh's first lessons in astral magic consisted mostly of various types of illusions. Beniss said they were the easiest and most natural talents to have come out. Eilidh could fool the eye, as well as the ear, and had learned to mask herself even better than her Watcher training had taught. She told Beniss about the blood faerie being able to contact her with some kind of mind-speak and that it had happened when Eilidh opened herself to astral flows. But Beniss said teaching her that would take too long. Mind-speaking was a difficult talent, one that would give them little advantage over what they would soon face.

They kept the plan simple. They would find the blood faerie and kill him. There would be no conversation, no negotiation, no attempts to reason with him. They had not arrived at the decision lightly, but with the help of the higher conclave, they concluded he would be impossible to restrain and unlikely to reform, especially if the Krostach Ritual had started to exact a price on the faerie's mind. Even if he were perfectly sane, they said, what faerie would be willing to give up magic? Eilidh shuddered as she realised she had nearly been willing to do just that to please Saor.

Every one of the azuri faeries would face death by the kingdom conclave, so it was no small thing for them to decide to take the life of someone whose crime was in his own magical talents. Yet the loss of four druids could not be tolerated. Bonding with a true druid went far beyond increasing a faerie's power.

Everyone, not least of all the higher conclave, had been shocked to learn that Munro had initiated the binding ceremony. That day in the woods when he'd said, *"Dem'ontar-che"* to Eilidh, he had unknowingly pledged his devotion. The fae on the

Isle of Skye had grown excited, telling Eilidh she already had his consent to bind him. Eilidh disagreed. She didn't know what magic had given him the words, but she would not let him cede his will to an incomprehensible magical force. The longer they were bonded, the more they would be inside each other's heads. It was not a thing to ask lightly.

Eilidh had to admit she was not certain about it either. She liked Munro, liked him very much. Her attraction for him had grown, despite everything she'd been taught about humans and fae. Not to mention that she found the possibility of mastering the Ways of Earth enticing. But to be so intimately aware of another person all the time, to have them etched into her mind, knowing there was no way to ever undo the ritual... Eilidh felt uncertain. Beniss seemed convinced that bonding with Munro would be vital to the success of finding and overcoming the blood faerie. Even knowing that, Eilidh would not complete the bond without his permission, not when she had so many doubts.

Although Eilidh wanted to get off the bus once they came to parts of the country that were more inhabited by humans, and therefore safer from fae Watchers, Beniss insisted they ride all the way to the city. They sat in the back, and Beniss did her best to teach Eilidh what she could. She drilled Eilidh over and over, often frustrated by how rigid Eilidh's mind had become after more than a century of resisting her talents.

As they came closer to Perth, Eilidh forgot how much she disliked the bus and its mechanical smells and grew nervous about seeing Munro. She had considered how she would explain the bonding. She knew most of the benefits would be hers. He would live longer, aging nearly as slowly as she did, but to a short-lived species, the idea of a centuries-long existence might not be appealing. Especially considering all of his friends, his family, everyone he loved would die while he lived on. According to Beniss and the higher conclave, Munro's magical abilities would probably not be enhanced. For him, the benefits were few, and the price might be more than he was willing to pay.

Finally, they arrived in the city. Eilidh was happy to run the few miles to Munro's house. Sitting for so long had made her legs ache and the movement helped clear her thoughts. Even the human smells of Perth were far more appealing than the enclosed air on the bus. She and Beniss ran, each step taking them closer to a conversation Eilidh was not quite ready to have. She told herself that she and Beniss would find a way to do what they must, even if Munro turned her down. But a place in her heart hoped he wouldn't. The feelings confused her. She couldn't put a name to them. They were certainly unlike the feelings she'd once had for Saor. When she told Beniss about it, Beniss said it was the power of the unfinished bonding ritual and that everything would become clear when the rite was complete.

Eilidh smiled in the warm summer evening as she approached Munro's neighbourhood. She realised how much she'd come to love the city and how much it felt like home. The higher conclave had urged her to return and complete her training, which could take many decades, but she had been reluctant to make promises. Someday she would, no doubt. The taste of casting the azure she'd gotten with Beniss left her hungry. But things were changing so fast. She wanted to be able to make commitments with a clear head, not in the shadow of peril.

When they finally arrived at Munro's house, Eilidh stopped in the front garden and stared at the door. Beniss reached down and took Eilidh's hand, giving it a gentle squeeze. "You must do this," she said.

"I know." Suddenly, all the things she planned to say abandoned her. She could feel him inside the house. He must have been aware of her too, but still she could not move.

The front door opened. Munro stood in the doorway. His eyes never left her. He did not even appear to notice Beniss or the fact that Eilidh's appearance had changed. He strode toward her and put his arms around her, pulling her into a fierce hug. He buried his face in her shoulder. Finally, after a long moment, he looked into her eyes. He started to speak, then instead, kissed her full on the mouth, with none of the indecision or hesitation he'd shown before. "Don't ever leave me again, Eilidh."

"You don't mean that," Eilidh said, turning her face away. "I have learned much since we last saw each other. These feelings you have for me are part of a bonding magic that we inadvertently triggered when we first met."

Munro put his finger on Eilidh's chin and tilted it upward to force her to meet his eyes. "I may not know a lot of things, but I know my own mind...and my own heart."

"Quinton, I have many things I need to tell you, but we don't have a lot of time." She squeezed his arm, and he released her.

He lowered his voice. "I know. We found two more bodies, probably his first victims, and I have reason to think he's killing druids. Although one of the first victims was likely fae."

Beniss and Eilidh exchanged a surprised look. The fae victim must have been an outcast, otherwise Saor would know of it. Eilidh nodded grimly. "We believe he is trying to perform what is known as the Krostach Ritual. It requires the hearts of four true druids."

Munro appeared to notice Beniss for the first time. "I assume you're not any more human than she is." He smiled and ran a finger over Eilidh's invisible twisted ear, causing her to shiver and blush.

"And you have doubts, child, that he wants to complete the life bond of a true druid servant?" Beniss asked with a smile.

"Servant?" For the first time since they'd arrived, uncertainty passed over Munro's face.

"If you consent to complete the bond with Eilidh, her strength will be increased many times over. She will gain access to magic that even one of her deep talents would have difficulty mastering on her own. Your connection with the Ways of Earth will be open to her, and she can use the powers to challenge the one who preys on your people. In exchange, you will receive the long life that fae enjoy and be forever bonded to the one you so obviously love."

Munro began to speak, but Eilidh held up a hand and stopped him from replying to Beniss. "There is more you should know. The bond is deep and cannot be severed. We will be in each other's minds and in each other's hearts as long as we both live. Should you change your mind…"

"I won't." His words were sure, but his voice held some hesitation.

"Quinton, you must…"

Munro held up a hand to stop her. He studied her eyes intently, then glanced to the sky. It was overcast, and Munro took some time and considered the clouds, breathing in the evening air. Finally, he spoke. "Do it. Whatever you have to."

This time it was Beniss who asked. "And the cost?"

"I'm not seeing a downside." Munro put a hand on either side of Eilidh's face. "The last two days as I felt you coming home, I've thought of little else than being with you. Do you love me? *Could* you love me?"

"These are not things the fae speak of." Eilidh felt her face reddening. She did not yet have the mastery of illusion to know if she kept it hidden.

"In case you haven't noticed, I'm not fae. If you bond with me, you'll have to get used to the fact that I'm not what you expect. I know things will take time, and I know we're different. But if you're asking me if it's too much to bear, being stuck with you for a very long time, the answer is no. It's not too much. Do what you have to do."

Eilidh glanced at Beniss, who nodded. The elder fae said, "Perhaps we could go inside?"

Munro led them into his house, and they sat awkwardly on the soft furniture. "I found this at the latest crime scene," Munro said, digging a small, carved stone out of his pocket. He handed it to Eilidh. It was beautiful work, more intricate than the rough shape she'd seen Munro make. "I made this the day you and Saor left," he said and gave her a small metal bear. In it, she could feel his essence, which had become as familiar as his face.

She showed both pieces to Beniss, who said, "The dead man was surely a druid. His heart was taken?"

"Yes. According to the coroner, he died before the other two. That means the blood faerie has taken three hearts, but one was destroyed. It looks like he tried to take the faerie's heart as well, but it was also found mangled at the scene. So whatever he tried didn't work there either."

Beniss grew pale. "An abomination," she said.

"While you were gone, I met a few other druids. I took your advice, Eilidh, and tracked down a cousin who seems to have a similar talent, although he's gifted with water, not stone. The druids talked about a mentor named Cridhe, but I don't know if he is a druid or fae."

Beniss tilted her head to one side. "It seems likely they are speaking of the blood faerie himself, although I do not know this name."

"Can any faerie detect a druid? My cousin seemed to know I was like him the moment I walked into his house."

"I do not think so. From what lore we still possess after our exile, it seems most azuri fae can only detect a druid with whom a bond would be successful. Not every druid is suited to every faerie. The magic is complex."

"Yes," Eilidh said. "The first time I saw Quinton, I knew there was something different about him." She remembered that night, how she watched Munro from the shadows and how he seemed to be able to sense her in the dark.

"I had not anticipated there would be more druids the blood faerie was keeping alive." Beniss seemed troubled. "How he has managed to collect so many is beyond me. True druids are so rare. He must be old and worked long and hard in his search, or possibly found a strong lineage."

"What do you mean?" Munro asked.

"It could be your blood connection to your cousin enabled him to sense your talents. As you will learn when you further your training with Eilidh, our heart and blood is the conduit for our magical flows."

"On the other hand," Eilidh remarked. "You and your people do not travel very much. Perhaps druids are not so rare as you thought."

"That was not always so. Only within the last thousand years has the kingdom conclave persecuted those who cast the azure. Although most of us are gone, Galen, Oron, and I are all from a time before. We remember when things were much different in the kingdom. Even before the persecution started, we sought out true druids, but few found one." Beniss looked pointedly at Munro. "And that was after a thousand years of searching. I cannot imagine how the blood faerie found so many. At least we know that until he completes the Krostach Ritual, he can only bond with one of them. The fae-druid bond can only happen one time in the lifespan of each. If we can determine which one is his creature, we target that one, and his death will weaken our foe."

Munro's eyes narrowed. "No. We're not killing anyone we don't have to." He looked from Beniss to Eilidh, his eyes determined.

"If he has bonded with a druid, it has increased his powers immensely. When the druid dies, the blood faerie's additional power will die with him. Besides, even if the druid survived, he would be useless to us, since he would not be able to bond with another." Beniss shrugged.

"I will have no part in killing an innocent man, and if you try, I will stop you. Cridhe is a ruthless murderer, and I have reconciled myself to the fact that I can't exactly arrest him. But as far as we know, the druids haven't committed any crimes or even been aware that Cridhe is responsible for the murders. Nobody, not even you, is going to go around killing innocent people. Make no mistake about that."

His passion stirred something within Eilidh. Although she saw the practicality of Beniss' words, she had seen too much killing of innocents. "Quinton is right. The only death we seek is that of Cridhe, the blood faerie."

Beniss relented with a brief nod of assent toward Munro.

"I forgot to mention, my cousin Frankie, the druid, asked me to come by tonight. I think he's starting to piece together what is going on, assuming he didn't already know. He might be willing to lead us to Cridhe. He hasn't admitted he knew all three victims, but it's unlikely he didn't. He and the others have to be getting worried."

Eilidh fingered the stone Munro had found at the crime scene. "Beniss, do you think this stone means the human victim was of stone talents?" She couldn't help but hope Munro would not be a target for the Krostach Ritual.

Beniss shook her head. "No, child." She reached over and touched the blackened grooves. "This was crafted with fire. A remarkable piece." She nodded at Eilidh. "I know your fears, and I share them. But even if this were a stone druid's work, we cannot be certain the dead man made it. Any of them could have dropped it."

Munro turned to Beniss. "How much sway will Cridhe have over the druids?"

"If you're asking about compulsion, that's unlikely with one of blood talents." She nodded toward Eilidh. "That's more along the line of our gifts. It's complicated and dangerous to both the one who casts it and the object of the incantation. I'm not as familiar as Oron with the rituals of the blood, but I do know casting the azure does not work the same way as invoking the Ways of Earth.

"The four earth talents are compatible. One faerie may have even some abilities in two or three of the seasons. With the Path of the Azure, not only are we restricted to one path, but talents in the Path tend to run in families. So every faerie in my lineage that has access to the Path only has gifts in astral magic. Blood sticks with blood, as they used to say. I could not cast blood shadows any more than I could breathe underwater." Beniss paused to think for a moment. "Although he probably has no control over their thoughts or access to their minds, he may have other ways of tracking them. The body, the blood, the bone, he will be able to manipulate these things with ease. If you share familial blood with one of his minions, you should be wary."

Munro glanced at his watch. "I have to go. Frankie's expecting me. I'll find out what he knows, and we'll decide what to do from there."

"The ritual must be completed," Beniss said.

Eilidh shook her head. "We are not ready. We will discuss it further when Munro comes home tonight." She appreciated his certainty about their bonding, but she couldn't yet share it.

Munro gave her a searching look, but he didn't press.

"I don't like the delay, but a few hours won't hurt. We should come with you," Beniss said.

"There's no way he'd talk around strangers. It's taken long enough for him to trust me, and I'm family. He's my cousin. I'll be fine. I don't know how deep he's in with Cridhe, but we're blood. Besides, he needs my help."

Eilidh started to argue, but Beniss placed her hand on Eilidh's arm and shook her head. "Let him go. We have things to discuss and plans to make."

Munro stood and took Eilidh's hand, helping her to her feet. As she slipped the carved stone into his palm, he kissed her lightly on the cheek. "I won't be long. Make yourself at home. I'll give you a ring if I have any trouble."

He left before Eilidh could ask him what that meant. There was so much she didn't understand about humans. Eilidh turned to ask Beniss what she planned to do next, but Beniss didn't give her the chance. "We'd better go. He'll probably drive, and we don't want to lose him."

"We're going to follow?" Eilidh asked.

"Don't be stupid. Of course we are."

∞

When Munro got to his car, he tapped on his mobile's touch-screen to call Frankie and tell him he was on his way. Instead of wanting to meet at his house, Frankie asked him to come to a farmhouse out by Abernethy. It wasn't too far, but it seemed an unusual request and Munro felt wary. Frankie explained that the place was owned by one of the other druids and he had persuaded them to meet with Munro.

Now that he knew others would be there, part of Munro wished he'd let Eilidh and Beniss come. It was too late to go back and ask, and he just wasn't sure how the druids would react to meeting faeries. Assuming they didn't know what Cridhe was. Although Eilidh and Beniss *looked* human, he could tell they weren't. He assumed the others would be able to sense the difference too.

The meeting was too important to risk spooking them. The best case scenario, in his mind, was to learn something of Cridhe's location, and what, if anything, Frankie and the others knew about him. If he could convince the others to turn against their mentor, that could make his job a lot easier. Munro didn't like the idea that, if he succeeded, the police would never know the truth. But if the killings stopped, that had to be enough for him.

By the time Munro exited the highway at Bridge of Earn and turned toward Abernethy, the long summer dusk had dissolved into darkness. He parked his car where Frankie had told him to and grabbed a torch. Flicking it on, he headed down a dirt track on foot. Soon he arrived at a cluster of abandoned outbuildings. It seemed like an odd meeting place, but on the other hand, he couldn't picture where in town a bunch of druids would get together to practice magic. This seemed as good a place as any.

Frankie stepped out of a feed barn. "There you are. Come on then. The others are waiting."

When Munro went into the barn, he saw Frankie was not alone. The man stood with an elegant disdain Munro had come to associate with the fae. But that wasn't the only reason Munro immediately knew his race. His ears were sharply pitched at the top, although not twisted like Eilidh's. His skin had a strange, blue-grey pallor Munro associated with the dead. He hadn't seen many dead bodies, but the ones he had were firmly stuck in his mind.

Munro froze. He knew exactly who this was. He felt a tingle of dread.

Frankie seemed visibly shaken and more than a little apologetic. "The others will be here soon. Meanwhile, our mentor wanted to meet you. This is Cridhe."

Frankie had set him up, and they both knew it. But had he been compelled, or did he do it willingly?

The blood faerie looked Munro up and down. "I can smell her on you."

Munro felt a small relief that they weren't going to pretend. He shrugged. Frankie, on the other hand, seemed puzzled. Obviously, Cridhe had not told his underlings about Eilidh. Interesting.

"I'm disappointed you didn't bring her with you. But never fear, I suspect she'll come for you soon enough. While we're waiting, I'd like to show you something." Cridhe turned to Frankie. "Wait for us."

Frankie gave a small awkward bow to Cridhe and left them alone.

Finally, Munro found his voice. "What makes you think Eilidh will follow me here?"

"The bond, of course. I had to figure out the bond on my own. Dudlach hid the truth from me for a time. If I had known, I never would have let him kill Jon. But now I understand, you see. Perhaps it is better this way." Cridhe went on, oblivious to Munro's confusion. "So I *know* that once she feels your pain, she'll come running. I do regret, however, that I have to kill you. I want you to understand that. The others, well, they were necessary and expendable. But your death will pain my future queen, and that is most regrettable. If only you were not gifted in stone." Cridhe shrugged, lifting his shoulders with perfect grace. He looked like an undead fashion model.

Munro glanced toward the door, an unwelcome knot of fear tightening in his stomach.

"Don't do that. It would be most tedious to have to chase you. I ordinarily don't mind a hunt, but I have much to do tonight. Here, I have something to show you." Cridhe gestured to an inner door. "After you."

When Munro was near Eilidh, and even Beniss, he felt a fine tugging that he supposed was a response to their magical nature. With Cridhe, the sensation was more like a claw grasping something within him. He didn't know if it was because of the difference between blood magic and astral magic, or if Cridhe had become twisted and warped through his murderous actions. The closer he got to Cridhe, the more Munro's stomach clenched. This answered one of his questions about Frankie and the other true druids. There was no way they could be around Cridhe and not realise something was very wrong with him.

It pained Munro to think it, but his cousin had sought the power Cridhe could give him and had ignored the obvious dangers. It didn't justify the death of Robert Dewar and the others, of course. But if they accepted his teaching, they had to have understood there would be a cost. They must have known Cridhe was responsible for the murders, but did they play a part?

Seeing no other option, Munro preceded Cridhe through the wooden door. They walked into a small room with no furniture or decoration. The only object was a wooden crate filled with straw.

"Please. Look inside."

Munro found the blood faerie's politeness peculiar. He intended to kill Munro, likely in the same gruesome way he had the others. And yet, he still took time to say things like *please*. Not that Munro planned to let Cridhe kill him. He hadn't yet tested the blood faerie's power, but the moment for rebellion hadn't come. He had to admit, he was curious about what Cridhe wanted to show him. A small part of him hoped Cridhe was right and Eilidh would show up before long.

What Cridhe didn't seem to know was that he and Eilidh had not yet bonded. Munro understood why Eilidh had been reluctant to bond herself with a human, but now he wished they had done it before he left. Munro had a feeling they would need the extra power before this thing was done. Now he feared it was too late. Munro didn't correct Cridhe's misapprehension, even though he wasn't sure what keeping that little titbit to himself would accomplish. On the other hand, he didn't see any point in telling Cridhe anything he didn't have to.

Munro approached the crate and swept aside some of the straw. As soon as his hand touched the stone tablet, he felt a jolt of power.

Cridhe smiled at Munro's reaction. "Impressive, isn't it?"

It took Munro a moment to clear away the straw from the tablet's surface. It was old. He could tell that easily enough by its appearance, but more than that, it had a strong and peculiar resonance. The tablet was something like the small objects he moulded with his hands, but the person who made it knew what he was doing and why. "This is druid made, isn't it?" He ran his finger lightly over the surface, concerned that his own power might mar it.

"I really am most disappointed that you have to die. You're much more clever than the others. And talent with stone is nearly as rare as fire. With you, I could create my own tablets, divine my own rituals." Cridhe tilted his head to one side, as though lost in thought. "Your cousin tells me you have managed to create objects of power. Did Eilidh guide you in this?"

Munro didn't want to give Cridhe any information about Eilidh or himself. He was under no illusion about how dangerous Cridhe was. He'd seen the bodies. On the other hand, if he could delay or distract him, that might be of some help. He only wished he had some way to warn Eilidh. He had his mobile, but he wasn't sure Eilidh would even know how to answer the phone.

Munro met Cridhe's eyes and shook his head. "She was as surprised as I was. Considering her situation, she doesn't know a lot about druids."

Cridhe looked Munro up and down as though evaluating whether Munro would try to deceive him. Munro couldn't tell what Cridhe perceived, but the blood faerie moved on. "If only I had been successful with Craig Laughlin. Then you wouldn't have to die. But as you can see, the rite demands a stone sacrifice."

Munro couldn't see, but he was not about to argue with the mad faerie. "If you don't mind me asking, where are their hearts?"

Cridhe smiled. "Don't worry. They are safe and beating strong."

At that moment Cridhe's power hit Munro full in the chest. It was like being kicked in the solar plexus by a horse. He fell backward, stunned and unable to speak.

"You won't be alone. After tonight, I don't think Frankie will be as willing as he has been in the past. So I think he's the best choice for our water sacrifice."

"And what of Laughlin? You failed with him; the heart was ruined. Are you certain that won't happen again?"

Cridhe tilted his head thoughtfully. "You're right. I should take Frankie first. If I fail with him, there are other water druids. Besides, you can't die until I'm certain Eilidh is on her way."

Munro felt sick at the thought of what was about to happen. He staggered to his feet and tried to lunge at Cridhe. The blood faerie easily deflected the stumbling attack.

"It's time."

CHAPTER 18

WHEN EILIDH HEARD MUNRO'S CAR pull away, she signalled Beniss that it was time to go. As soon as she went out the front door, her senses were overcome with the smell of the Otherworld. Four kingdom fae stepped out of the shadows, led by Saor. Beniss hissed and moved into a defensive crouch.

"Peace, Beniss. We're here to help," Saor said. "The conclave agrees something must be done about the outcast."

"All of the outcasts?" Eilidh said. "Are you here to *do something* about me too?" She could no longer hide her bitterness. The more she'd thought about it, the more it annoyed her that Saor had asked her to give up her magic. He wanted her to become a shell of herself so she could fit within his world and become acceptable to those around him. After only a few days of training and talking with Beniss, Eilidh realised that being *acceptable* wasn't worth the price.

Judging by the anger on his face, Saor knew things were never going to be as he always thought they should be. "If you recall, Eilidh, it was you who requested our help."

Beniss nodded to one of Munro's neighbours, who had come out of his house and was openly staring at the group. Although the sky had grown darker, the soft leather clothing and piercing eyes of Saor and his companions, who did not have the ability to appear human, were attracting attention. "We should take this discussion inside."

Eilidh looked sharply at Beniss. "But what of Munro?"

"Can you not feel him?"

"I can..." Eilidh could not explain why she felt uneasy. It could be that she and Munro had left things unfinished, or perhaps it was simply the uncertainty of what they were about to do. Her training sessions with Beniss made her realise how little she really knew. Sure, she could cast an illusion, but that didn't always mean controlling and maintaining it. The blood faerie they were dealing with, Cridhe, obviously had decades if not centuries of experience. Beniss was old, and therefore her experience would be invaluable, but she admitted she did not relish the idea of challenging a blood faerie with a bonded druid. Truth be told, she'd been hoping for more from the conclave. Although Saor was a good warrior, he was nearly as young as she. Even with four companions, she feared they would not be any match for the blood faerie.

"Inside," Beniss said firmly. "This is not the place."

Eilidh felt a slight pressure inside her mind. It didn't hurt, but it was enough to remind her that Beniss was her elder and deserved respect. Eilidh acquiesced with a slight inclination of her head. "As you wish." She didn't feel any better about the situation, but she needed Beniss if she had any hope of stopping Cridhe. She also recognised that Munro could take care of himself. Although she wanted to know what his cousin would report about Cridhe's location and plans, if Munro trusted Frankie, then she must as well.

The six entered Munro's house. Eilidh didn't know Saor's companions. They were young, perhaps even younger than Saor, and they seem distinctly uncomfortable. Saor gestured to her ears and face. "I see you have mastered some illusion at least." With an almost imperceptible sneer he added, "It suits you." If she had not known him so well, she would not have realised how embittered he had become in such a short time. She steeled herself to ignore the slight. She'd made her choice, and she had to accept the consequences.

Beniss looked squarely at Saor. "What is the conclave's plan?"

"Eilidh knows the most about the one we seek. It is generally agreed that she should help us find and eliminate the threat." His tone indicated he was not one of those who agreed.

"Munro is going to lead us to him. He has discovered someone who is in the blood faerie's inner circle. He has gone to meet with him now." Eilidh could not resist showing Saor that a human would be the key to finding their target.

Although Saor had schooled his features, Eilidh could tell the remark hit home. "Then why are you here?"

"We were about to follow when the four of you showed up."

"We will accompany you." Saor's tone left no room for argument.

Although Eilidh's instinct said he should not come, the nagging worry for Munro's safety told her pride was not worth it. She opened her mouth to reply when her connection with Munro disappeared. She grabbed Beniss' arm and staggered slightly. "Beniss..." She used all of her newly developed magical senses to search, but it was as though he had never existed.

"What is wrong, child?"

"He's gone."

"What do you mean?" Beniss' voice was sharp, and the illusion that held her pretty human face faltered for a moment.

The room spun slightly and Eilidh touched the arm of a chair to maintain her balance. "I don't know what happened. I could feel him in my mind like always, but then he was just gone." Panic tightened her chest and grief threatened to overwhelm her. "Is he..." Her voice trailed off. She couldn't bring herself to think the worst.

Beniss put her hands on either side of Eilidh's face. "Eilidh, gather yourself. Even though you did not complete the ritual, I believe you would know if he was dead. Something else is stopping you from being able to sense him." The elder faerie's expression softened. "Now you must complete the ritual. You must accept his bond. That should help you cut through whatever trickery has hidden him from you."

Eilidh hesitated. Once she did this, there was no turning back. Faeries were not good at forever. It probably came from having long lives. Only the royals tended to mate for life, but their arrangements were more for political and social standing than for love or even the hope of producing children. But according to Beniss, the druid bond was permanent. Thanks to its power, Munro's life span could be as long as hers.

She asked herself a question, because she had to. Was stopping the blood faerie worth jumping into a lifelong bond with a human she had just met? Yes, it would increase her power, but she tried not to consider that. She couldn't treat Munro like merely a vessel. As she considered the deep loss she'd felt when she'd lost contact with him, Eilidh realised she was wasting time. "What do I have to do?"

Beniss patted Eilidh softly on the cheek. "Good. Most would search a lifetime to find someone willing and able to take the bond. Not every druid is compatible with every faerie. What Munro has agreed to must always be honoured."

She continued to search Eilidh's eyes, and Eilidh felt pressure in her mind, as though Beniss was searching her thoughts. She started to resist. "What are you doing?"

"Searching for the strand."

Eilidh didn't know what she meant, but now was not the time to argue. Beniss might look like a human teenager, but she was a fae of some power. Suddenly, Eilidh felt a sharp call in her mind.

"Good. You feel that. Now make your vow."

At first, Eilidh didn't know what to say, then she recalled what Munro had said to her in the woods— the phrase that initiated the ritual in the first place. *Dem'ontar-che.* Loyalty, faith, devotion. How he had known to say those words? It was magic far beyond her understanding, but the bond they were about to solidify must have reached them both on an instinctual level. Eilidh looked at Saor and could not help but silently speak words of regret.

Pushing that aside, Eilidh closed her eyes and thought of nothing but Quinton Munro. She pictured his face, let her nose take in the scent of him that still lingered in his house, let her ears echo with the sound of his voice, and felt his kiss on her lips. "*Dem'ontar-che.*" Eilidh expected a flash, a feeling of rightness, some magical display of lights or something. But nothing happened. She opened her eyes, looked at Beniss, and shook her head. "Is there something else I need to do?"

"Now, we wait."

Saor huffed with impatience. "How long will this take?"

Beniss let her human facade melt away, and Saor saw the elder faerie's true face. Her voice rolled like thunder. "Quiet, earth faerie. We're not in the kingdom now." To Eilidh she said, "Magic is not a machine. It takes as long as it takes."

∞

"He's going to kill us both," Munro said to Frankie as Cridhe led him out of the building to meet the others.

"I know." Frankie sounded resigned.

Munro's anger burst out. "Why would you do this? I'm family." He'd never felt so betrayed. "You could have talked to me. We would have helped you."

"We?"

There was no reason for the other druids not to know about Eilidh now. Munro opened his mouth to answer, but before he could speak, a burning fire filled his throat. He could hear it crackle and taste the smoke. It took a moment for the pain to hit, but when it did, his whole world came undone. Frankie screwed his eyes shut as Munro screamed. He stood, clenching his fists by his side.

Munro held his hands around his own neck, unable to stop from crying out with the pain. He looked at his cousin and croaked, "Please. Help me."

Frankie glanced around the old farm buildings where they stood. The place had been abandoned for some time, and there was not much of use lying around. Frankie spotted a stack of wood from busted-up fencing. He grabbed a board and rushed at Munro, striking him on the side of the head.

Munro sank to the ground. The last thing he saw as he drifted into unconsciousness was Cridhe smiling. "That should get my queen's attention," the mad faerie said. "Now as for you..." Munro heard no more. His last thought before he blacked out was that he hoped Eilidh had not felt any of it. If it meant she had been protected from the pain, he was grateful she hadn't completed the ritual after all.

He drifted in and out for what felt like hours, but may have been just minutes. At least the fire in his throat had been quenched. He still felt pain, and he wasn't sure he could speak. A scream, this time not his own, grabbed his attention. It was only then Munro realised he was lying on the ground and not in the same place where he'd lost consciousness. They were in a small clearing in the woods. A few feet away lay Frankie. Cridhe crouched over him, a vile, greasy incantation slipping from his mouth. Munro felt the ancient magic through his own clouded thoughts.

Frankie stopped screaming. From a gory cavity in his chest, Cridhe lifted out Frankie's heart. Cridhe's incantation ceased, and in the silence of the night, Munro clearly heard the thump-thumping of his cousin's heart as it rested in the blood faerie's hand.

"Come, Dudlach. Let us put Frankie in his place," Cridhe said to the empty air. His eyes glistened with power and exertion. His once-grey face was now flushed with a rosy glow. Cridhe turned to Munro. "Don't worry. We won't be long."

The blood faerie left, leaving Munro dazed and in pain. He struggled to rise, then only managed to stagger around. He tried not to stare at his cousin's body, as he reeled in the opposite direction from the one Cridhe had gone. As soon as he reached the edge of the clearing, his body became weak, as though he was bleeding out, even though he didn't have any serious cuts. His head screamed with pain, but there was only a small amount of blood. When Munro stepped closer to the centre of the clearing, the sensation passed. Munro cursed under his breath. Why had he not let Eilidh accompany him? He should have seen this coming. Although he wanted to believe he would have made different choices had he been in Frankie's place, seeing Cridhe's power and the ruthlessness with which he wielded it, Munro knew no human could stand against it.

He reached for his pocket, only to find his mobile was gone. A feeling of despair settled over him, and he could not help but look at Frankie's face and the horror on his lifeless features. The same fate awaited him as soon as Cridhe got back, and he couldn't do anything about it.

He closed his hand around the small carved stone in his pocket. Why did druids make these things? Did they hold power? Did they serve a purpose? He didn't even know how they were crafted, much less what they were supposed to do, so how could he even think to use it?

Munro recalled that Beniss had said if they took out Cridhe's bonded druid, the blood faerie would be much less powerful. He hoped Cridhe's earlier ramblings meant his bonded druid was already dead, possibly the first victim, the one they'd found with the dead faerie. Could this be his stone? But who had the faerie been? And would this mean Cridhe was truly weaker? He didn't seem weak to Munro.

Cridhe returned much sooner than Munro expected and saw that Munro was fully awake and walking around. He made a gesture with one blood-stained hand and Munro crumpled to the ground, unable to move or even struggle. "Now you can explain to me, druid, why my queen did not come running to your aid. No fae would turn her back on her bonded druid. The magic would not let them."

Although it was a small and shallow victory, Munro felt a certain sense of triumph. He laughed even though the burns in his throat hurt. His voice came out in a horrific rasp. "There is no bond. I initiated, but she refused."

Cridhe's face contorted with anger. "That is not possible. What faerie would refuse a bonding when it means so much more power? She must come. I had it all planned. She will arrive and see me at the apex of my power. Once she has me, your death will seem but a minor inconvenience. She will be content to live in the glow of what the Krostach Ritual will provide."

Cridhe continued to mutter and pace. He took his attention away from Munro, and the bonds loosened, allowing Munro to relax his muscles. Lying there in the dirt, a sudden, cool relief began to spread through Munro's throat. He couldn't understand what was happening. Although it wouldn't surprise him if Cridhe had the ability to heal him, he couldn't imagine why he would. Munro began to feel stronger, sharper, and the despair and fear melted away. Then he recognised what had been missing since Frankie hit him on the head. *Eilidh.*

When Munro looked up, he found Cridhe watching him intently, a smile quirked on his face. "It appears she did not refuse after all." Cridhe gazed north and whispered, "Hurry, my queen. I'm growing impatient."

CHAPTER 19

MUNRO KNEW EILIDH had somehow completed the bond. Before, he'd felt her presence as a vague awareness. Now he saw her in his mind's eye, and he knew she was coming. Her emotions swept over him, more than he would have thought her cool demeanour would allow. He'd thought her introspective and passionless, but now he knew she felt emotions intensely. She could likely feel him as well, and he wondered how she would judge him, if she would come to regret fusing her soul with his.

Thoughts drifted through his mind with a twinge of sorrow, because he understood what he would lose when he died. Still, the thoughts weren't enough to distract him from the pulsing darkness around him. He felt singular dread as Cridhe came toward him, knowing Eilidh would be too late.

"She certainly is taking her time. I suppose it's natural for her to be caught up in a new bonding. She really should have completed it some time ago. Poor planning, really." Cridhe crouched over Munro. "It's an honour for you to be the final sacrifice. Fitting. I shall consider it a tribute to my queen, that the sacrifice of her bonded druid will be the beginning of our reign."

"Do you really think you'll be so powerful that you can take on the kingdom fae alone? How many of them are there? Tens of thousands? Hundreds of thousands?" Munro didn't know how realistic Cridhe's plan was, but Beniss and Eilidh seemed to take the threat seriously. All he could hope to accomplish was to plant a seed of doubt. "What of the azuri fae at the Isle of Skye? What if they challenge you? Eilidh told me there were hundreds of them, maybe more. Even if the kingdom fae aren't a threat, wouldn't that many other azuri fae be a worry?" Munro felt desperate. He tried to think of anything that might make Cridhe take a moment to think. The more he could distract him, the better the chance Eilidh would arrive before things got any uglier.

Cridhe didn't stop what he was doing. Ever since he'd killed Frankie, his eyes shone with power. Or perhaps it was madness, or a combination of the two. With an easy flick of the hand, he tore open Munro's shirt, exposing his chest.

Munro's heart pounded as fear gripped him. Cridhe stared intently at Munro's chest, as though able to see through the skin, directly to his heart. "It won't do any harm, I suppose, just to get you ready."

Cridhe peered into the dark woods, and then grumbled, disappointed. "She really should be here by now," he repeated. He turned his attention back to Munro and ran a finger over his bare skin.

Munro felt a deep slicing burn everywhere the finger traced. He looked down and saw blood welling as Cridhe pushed the muscles aside. With a flick of the faerie's finger, a rib snapped. Nausea swept over Munro. He wanted nothing more than to lose consciousness, to escape in darkness, but he knew he had to fight. When another rib snapped, he cried out, his throat still burning. Sweat poured over his skin, mingling with rivulets of blood.

He tried to keep his attention on the stone in his hand. He felt warmth coming from it, perhaps from the fire magic that had crafted it. But he could do nothing more. Despair overwhelmed him.

His new bond with Eilidh meant his body was healing itself, a side effect of the bonding Munro had not anticipated. But Cridhe, rather than being angry, seemed fascinated, and the healing made things worse. When Cridhe saw what was happening, he broke ribs in a third place and then a fourth, creating a circular pattern around Munro's heart. The healing kept Munro alive and conscious, but it didn't stop the pain.

Munro dropped the stone, and it immediately drew Cridhe's attention. One tear at a time slid down the blood faerie's face. "Jon," he said softly.

It took a moment for Munro to understand. Even as he prepared to kill again, Cridhe grieved for his bonded druid. "Jon was the first, wasn't he?" Munro forced out the words through gritted teeth. "The one we found at Comrie? You killed him?"

Cridhe shook his head. "I didn't kill you, Jon. Dudlach knew I wouldn't give you up, so he killed you first. We needed a fire druid for the Krostach Ritual. And in all his searching, even with his special talent for detecting dormant druids, Dudlach only found one. You." Cridhe got a distant expression on his face, and for the moment, stopped breaking Munro's ribs. "It has a nice symmetry, now that I think of it. We began with you, my bonded druid, and end with my queen's druid. We both have made a deeper sacrifice than anyone could understand." His madness muddied his thoughts. Munro felt true hopelessness. The faerie seemed to think he was Jon and Munro, all rolled into one.

Suddenly, rustling noises came from the woods. It sounded as though help had finally arrived and brought an army with it. Cridhe leapt into a crouch, turning his head quickly from side to side, peering into the darkness. "My queen. Have you come to claim your place at my side? Watch then, as the era of glory begins." Cridhe extended a hand toward Munro, and Munro's heart started to pound in his chest. Munro screamed as Cridhe peeled back one of his broken ribs.

A hundred fae warriors stepped into view, all wielding knives and moving in perfect unison. "Stop!" Eilidh thundered, her voice coming from every direction and echoing like a storm. She stepped to the edge of the clearing, her eyes fastened on Cridhe.

Cridhe frowned, puzzled. "We need his heart, my queen. Krostach demands it." But the blood faerie smiled as though he understood. "Sacrifice is difficult for all of us." He glanced at Munro. "I love Jon too. No…" He shook his head, as though trying to maintain a grip on which druid he was killing. "We must be strong and set an example for our people."

"We have no people!" Eilidh shouted with ferocity.

Rage contorted Cridhe's features. He looked around, noticing the warriors for the first time. "You would bring kingdom Watchers against me? Eilidh, what have you done? You will find I can be a gentle and loving mate to you…or not. Do not try my patience."

He pointed at the warriors one after the other, and Munro could sense the power he directed at them. Shock passed over his face as each winked out of existence. "You would try to battle me with illusions?" His expression darkened. "Very well. You have made your choice."

Throughout the exchange, Cridhe did not release his magical grip on Munro's heart. It beat wildly, as though straining to be exposed and wanting to leap into Cridhe's hand. Munro's world faded. He fought to hold on, knowing that as long as he lived, Eilidh would be stronger. She needed that strength if she was to survive. Munro couldn't bear to think what it would mean if Cridhe had his way. His evil was horrific enough, but his madness was terrifying. With that last sorrowful thought, Munro plunged into darkness.

∞

Cridhe sent pulses of dark energy toward each of the shadow warriors, just as Eilidh expected he would. One at a time, they disappeared. But with each disappearance, Eilidh focused and cast the azure, causing a new illusory figure to take its place. Cridhe growled with frustration.

It sapped her energy in a way magic never had. But she'd never cast anything powerful before she met Beniss and the other azuri fae. Even now, if Beniss had not been using a mental link to refresh her energy, Eilidh didn't know if she could have maintained the constant multiple illusions. They had planned to test Cridhe's strength, to distract him, and as long as possible, to hide Beniss' presence.

Cridhe's frustration caused him to lash out, knocking back all of the illusion warriors in one huge sweep of his arm. Every time he did it, Eilidh brought up a new set. Cridhe pointed a finger at Eilidh. "Do not make me hurt you. *Do not be like her.*"

Eilidh couldn't help but wonder who he was talking about. Cridhe was clearly insane, so they might never know. He had some plan to make her his queen, thinking that together they would challenge the kingdom fae. She'd never seen such madness in one of their race. Many would have denied it was even possible, saying that such malady of the mind was the province of the weaker races, but dabbling with the dark Krostach ritual had exacted a price. While it repulsed her, it also made her sad, and a little afraid.

Cridhe stepped toward Eilidh and stopped just feet in front of her. His deathly, contorted face looked angry. It wouldn't require much more prodding for him to snap and strike her down. It took all her strength and focus to hold the illusion that made her appear cool and unperturbed. Because of their bond, only Munro could have known of the turmoil within her. The bond told her he still lived, but she didn't know for how long.

It was time to act. Eilidh raised a hand and flicked her wrist. Four more warriors stepped out of the woods.

"Must we continue to play these games?" Cridhe sighed, as though tired of indulging her.

Cridhe had not noticed these warriors were different. Saor and his three companions lifted their hands in unison. Eilidh felt a half smile tug at her mouth.

As one, the four warriors shouted an ancient word of power. From each of their hands came a blaze of green light. They struck Cridhe as one, and the blood faerie staggered back, a betrayal searing across his features. He was hit hard, and huge, gaping cuts appeared on his body. But he manipulated the flows of blood magic, and the bleeding was hastily staunched.

Cridhe lashed out with his power, the full force of his anger behind it. He traded shots with the earth warriors, but they were no match for his strength, experience, and cunning. He shouted a final incantation at them. Eilidh heard a sickening snap of bones. They tried to dodge, but his magic followed as they leapt aside. Eilidh's heart sank as two crumpled completely. Saor and the one closest to him were able to release one more spell before Cridhe retaliated with a final death blow.

The warriors had failed, and the time had come for Beniss to begin their attack of last hope. A cacophony of sounds blasted from every direction. Beniss stopped feeding Eilidh energy and cast a whirlwind of confusing sounds, voices, angry glowing lights. The nearby trees growled and twisted their many arms toward Cridhe. Even Eilidh had difficulty maintaining her nerve. Then the real onslaught began. Beniss stepped into the clearing from behind Eilidh, focusing intently on Cridhe. The elder faerie's magic thrummed.

Beniss had explained what she would do, even though the magic was far beyond what Eilidh could even begin to form. Eilidh had not appreciated the power and destruction such a spell might bring. For an astral faerie, the realm of strength was in the mind, and the mind of Cridhe must have been a terrible place. For around him began to spring up nightmares, embodiments of those he had killed, but also more gruesome things. Dark, daemonic creatures like Eilidh had never imagined. The nightmares turned on Cridhe, opening great maws toward him, clicking hideous mandibles.

Cridhe sent out spells of great power in every direction, attempting to fight things that were not there. As with Eilidh's warriors, when he would defeat one nightmare, another would take its place. Then Cridhe did something unexpected. Even Eilidh didn't believe she had the mental strength to do what he did, but Cridhe gathered all of his power and ignored the nightmares even as they began to attack and devour him. He looked directly at Beniss with all the hate and malice a faerie of his ability could possess, and he uttered one word, "Boil."

Although it appeared to drain Cridhe, his spell hit home. Beniss' skin turned red as a cherry, and she bled from every pore. She glanced over her shoulder and met Eilidh's eyes. Tears of blood streaked down her face. The nightmares around Cridhe exploded and disappeared as she died, her blood splattering in every direction.

Grief overwhelmed Eilidh as three of the people she cared most about lay dead or dying at her feet. Their plan had been for Saor to annoy and distract Cridhe, Eilidh to tire him, while Beniss finished him off with his own nightmares. His blood magic made him difficult to kill with physical force, and they thought his greatest weakness would be the mind. But his insanity provided him with a shroud of protection.

Only Eilidh was left to fight, and she only had one weapon left, one chance, even though it would cost her most dearly. She looked to Munro and said, "Forgive me." Although she could not be sure he could still understand her, she hoped he knew how much he had come to mean to her and that she did not make the sacrifice lightly.

She began to draw from him. Their bond gave her access to the earth magic that had always eluded her. She drank in his essence, knowing that as she did, she also took what little strength he had left.

As the connection deepened, Eilidh felt the power welling within her. Everything before had happened quickly, but now Eilidh felt the world slow. The trees surrounding the clearing stood on their roots. His battle with Beniss had drained Cridhe, but he was not yet done. He lifted a hand to bat away the illusions, and a shock spread over his face as he realised it was no illusion. Rocks rose off the ground and hurtled at him. Lightning flashed, and thunder sounded with a hollow boom. A ring of fire sprouted in the clearing.

For the first time, fear appeared on the blood faerie's face. As one unit, four trees lurched forward, trapping Cridhe in a wooden embrace. Eilidh screamed at Cridhe as she felt Munro's life force begin to dwindle and the power he lent her waned. "Damn you!" A string of ancient fae words flew from her lips. Each incantation sent tongues of fire at Cridhe. The sounds he made as he died would haunt Eilidh for centuries.

Eilidh went to her knees, exhausted. She never imagined it was possible to harness so much power, or lose so much in so short a time. All was still, and Eilidh wept.

CHAPTER 20

"GET THE BOLT CUTTERS after that gate. We'll need an ambulance all the way up here."

"What the hell happened here? Who are these people?"

"Eilidh? Is that you?"

"Can you hear me?"

"He's alive."

"Madam, you need to let us help him."

"*Dem'ontar-che.*"

A mask was fitted over Munro's face, sending cool sweet air into his lungs. Voices continued to drift in and out.

He was lifted and handled, but he did not have the strength or desire to fight them. He heard Hallward and Getty in the crowded mix of voices. All he could think about was how he would explain things. He tried to speak, but a man's voice said, "Calm down, son. Everything's okay now. You're going to be all right." Munro stopped fighting. He didn't know what he would have said anyway.

He opened his eyes. He was inside an ambulance. Eilidh was nowhere in sight, but he could sense her. She was tired and grieving, but alive, and that was more than he had hoped for.

Before Munro could refuse, the paramedic said, "Quick scratch," and injected something into his arm. Within seconds, Munro's pain and confusion eased. Warm darkness enveloped him.

When he opened his eyes again, he blinked at the glaring lights in a hospital room. Eilidh sat by his side in her human guise, muttering words in a language he did not understand. Getty was there too, sprawled across two uncomfortable-looking wooden chairs and covered by a hospital blanket.

Munro smiled, tentatively at first, and then more widely when he realised he didn't hurt. When Eilidh opened her eyes and smiled at him, warmth spread through his body.

"Quinton."

He loved the way she said his name. "What day is it?" he asked.

"The Equinox passed seven moonrises ago."

Munro laughed, suddenly not caring what day it was, happy to be alive. The memory of what had been done to him came crashing back. He lifted a hand to his chest. He was surprised to find no bandages, only skin rippled with twisted scars. "But..."

"It turns out the azuri fae were mistaken when they said there would be little benefit to you from the bonding. Everyone is astonished at how well you have healed, including me. I feared I had taken all of your strength. I thought you might not come back." A single tear slid down her rosy cheek.

"Hey, now. None of that." He wiped the tear away with his thumb. "You'll have to fill me in on what happened. I seem to have passed out." He grinned. "Sorry about that. I wasn't much use."

Eilidh knitted her eyebrows together. "Quinton, that isn't true. I could not have defeated the blood faerie without your strength and without your earth magic. The words were mine, but the power was yours." Once she seemed reassured that Munro was taking enough of the credit for the magic that had put an end to Cridhe, she went over the details, filling in the blank spots where he could not remember or had not been aware. When she came to the end of the story, Munro realised Getty had woken up and was listening intently.

"That's some story," Getty said, and hesitated as though choosing his words carefully. "It's the sort of thing a man would be tempted to not believe. I wouldn't have believed it if I hadn't seen the things I saw. The bodies, they weren't..."

"Human," Munro finished for him. "I know. It was hard for me to believe at first too."

Getty cast a furtive glance at Eilidh, as though he were afraid to meet her eyes. "You look different."

Eilidh smiled and wrinkled her nose. When she did, the illusion of humanity disappeared, but only for a moment. After the flash of reality, her curly ears became rounded again, and she again appeared human once more.

Getty gasped with surprise. He seemed as though he still wasn't quite ready to accept that some things were not as they appeared. Munro understood the feeling.

"What's the official word about all of this?" Munro couldn't imagine the report on what happened at Abernethy.

"You should have seen Hallward." Getty grinned. "He took it all in stride, like seeing *unusual* people, fireballs, and human sacrifice was an everyday thing. I hate to imagine what it would take to rattle that guy." Getty turned serious. "It was Frankie who called me, you know. It didn't make a lot of sense at the time, him calling from your phone. He was pretty panicked. But he said you were in trouble and we should bring the cavalry. He also said it was all his fault."

"He must have taken my phone after he hit me in the head with that damned plank."

"What'd he do that for?" Getty looked baffled.

"Cridhe, that was the blood faerie's…the killer's name, had just cast a spell that lit a fire in my throat. Literally. I guess it was the only thing Frankie could think of—knocking me out. It did the trick though, because Cridhe stopped after that."

"The blood…" Getty couldn't finish.

"Faerie. I know. Didn't Eilidh explain everything?"

Getty nodded at her. "She tried."

"They did not seem to believe me." Eilidh frowned.

Munro grinned. "I can understand that. I hardly believe it myself."

"I should call Hallward," Getty said. "He wanted to know as soon as you woke up. The official report says it was some kind of nutter cult that did the killings. The media is all in a frenzy, of course, but at least it has them looking in the wrong direction. I've seen all kinds of so-called experts on cults and Satanism on the BBC ever since the media officer released a statement."

"I suppose Hallward will be bitching that I'm not at work," Munro said with a laugh. "He never has approved of sick leave, and I think I've taken more in the last month than I have my entire time on the job."

"I wouldn't worry too much," Getty said. "I think having your heart almost ripped out by a *cult* is enough to warrant some time off. Hell, you could probably retire on medical disability if you wanted to."

"I'm not sure what I want to do. Part of that will depend on Eilidh."

Getty stood. "I'd best leave you two to discuss it then." He said goodbye and promised to visit Munro again soon.

Eilidh looked toward the door. "I do not think he believes us still."

Munro chuckled. "I think he's trying. I'm not in a straightjacket, so that's a start." He smiled at Eilidh. Because of the bond, he could sense her emotions. She was relieved and even relaxed, but he also detected apprehension. "What else is bothering you?"

"I have a difficult journey to make. After Cridhe's death, I received word from the conclave. They observed what happened in the woods. They said because I fought against the blood faerie and defended Saor and his companions, they would welcome me again into the Halls of Mist."

Munro expected such news would make her happy, but Eilidh seemed distinctly sad. He waited for her to continue.

"Saor would have been so pleased. It was all he would have wanted. I could have returned, and we could have been together."

The thought of Eilidh with Saor sent a stab of pain through Munro, but then he realised what she'd said. "Saor didn't make it?"

"None of them survived. Only you and I remain. If it had not been for our bond, we would not have lived."

"Then we have a lot to be grateful for. So you loved him?"

"Once, yes. Things changed, and I think he even had grown to hate me. It breaks my heart that the last words we spoke were angry ones. Still, I should attend his death rite, now that I'm permitted to. I hope I can convince the conclave to change their minds about the azuri fae. Since they see that my astral magic and our bond saved them from many losses, if not a total collapse of the kingdom, perhaps they will realise how unjust they have been. It would be nice to be able to tell Beniss' family they could rejoin the kingdom." She looked down. "I will have to spend some time considering the proper words to tell them of her bravery in death."

"I'd like to come with you to Saor's funeral." Munro didn't know if it would be appropriate, but he felt he should offer.

Eilidh smiled. "Thank you. I have to do this alone."

Munro wanted to say he understood, but he stayed silent. At least with the bond, he knew Eilidh sensed what he felt.

"I do hope you will come to the Isle of Skye with me. I may be there for some time. I have a lot to learn. Once I have learned more about the Path of the Azure, it will be time for us to work together to refine my understanding of the Ways of Earth. If, that is, you do not regret what we have done."

"We did the only thing we could do. But no, I do not regret it. Eilidh, I love you."

He could feel the uncertainty in her thoughts, but they melted away as she smiled. "My people are not as hasty as yours. For us, love is not a word we often use. My father said once that we are shallow and vain people." She touched his hand. "I feel for you something I have never felt before, Quinton. We have a lifetime to discover what words to use." She leaned over and softly touched his lips with hers.

After a moment of silence she said, "I'll return after Saor's death ritual, and we can travel to the Isle of Skye together."

Munro nodded and grinned. "I'm afraid we'll have to drive. I can't run as long or as fast as you can."

Eilidh groaned and leaned over, resting her forehead on Munro's shoulder. "We're going to have to work on that. You may grow stronger and faster over time."

He kissed her hair. "A lot of changes are coming our way." Part of him felt a loss, not just for the death of his cousin, Saor, Beniss, and the others, but for the old life he feared he couldn't go back to. Yet even though he had been satisfied with his life, he had been alone. Now he would never be alone again.

Eilidh didn't answer, but she didn't have to. Beyond her tiredness, her grief, and concerns for the future, he also felt the underlying contentment in her heart. Amidst the pain, they'd found each other, and that was something worth holding on to.

A NOTE FROM THE AUTHOR

Thank you so much for reading Blood Faerie, the first book in the Caledonia Fae series. If you enjoyed it, please take a moment to leave a review at your favourite online retailer.

I welcome contact from readers. At my website, you can contact me, sign up for my newsletter to be notified of new releases, read my blog, and find me on social networking.

—India Drummond

Author website: http://www.indiadrummond.com
Reader email: author@indiadrummond.com

THE CALEDONIA FAE SERIES

Book 1: Blood Faerie

Unjustly sentenced to death, Eilidh ran—away from faerie lands, to the streets of Perth, Scotland. Just as she has grown accustomed to exile, local police discover a mutilated body outside the abandoned church where she lives. Recognising the murder as the work of one of her own kind, Eilidh must choose: flee, or learn to tap into the forbidden magic that cost her everything.

Book 2: Azuri Fae

A faerie prince disappears in the borderlands, and his father enlists the help of outcast Eilidh and her bonded druid, Quinton Munro. Tantalised with hints of a lost and ancient magic, they learn that time is working against them every step of the way. Is the prince's disappearance related to the vanishing of an entire Scottish village?

Faced with deception, assassination attempts, and a mad queen who would sacrifice her own child to keep a dreaded secret, Eilidh struggles with an impossible situation. Her people demand she commit treason and betray the man she loves. Will she do what duty requires, or throw away the chance to reunite the kingdom in exchange for the life she hadn't dared hope for?

Book 3: Enemy of the Fae

With a young, inexperienced monarch on the Caledonian throne and traitorous plots implicating those nearest Queen Eilidh, unrest is rife in the kingdom. She must sift through the intrigues and lies to survive, all while trying to discover which of her trusted companions hates her enough to commit mass murder.

Pressures threaten to overcome the young ruler, and to protect Quinton Munro, her bonded druid, she must send him away. His journey becomes a mission when he stumbles on an ancient truth that will shake the foundations of the entire faerie realm. Confronted by infinite danger and the promise of limitless power, Munro faces the most difficult choices of his life. Will he hide the truth to preserve stability in the faerie kingdoms or embrace the promise of his true druid heritage?

One friend will die because of that truth, one friend's betrayal will cause irreparable scars, and the once tightly-knit band of druids will learn that not all magic is benevolent.

Book 4: Druid Lords

The druids of Caledonia have taken their place in the Halls of Mist, only to learn that their path is fraught with many dangers. When their newest member, Huck Webster, finds a woman of magical talents in Amsterdam, their troubles multiply. Lying between them and a peaceful existence are a dead prince, a furious queen, and a druid accused of murder. Each druid must search his soul and discover where his talents, and his loyalties, lie.

Book 5: Elder Druid

As the Druid Hall celebrates the completion of the Mistgate, their leader Munro is abducted, leaving them in disarray. Queen Eilidh declares Munro dead, which threatens the fragile balance of power in the Halls of Mist. With the druids crippled by grief and uncertainty, no one notices the insidious force influencing them from a dark mirror realm.

That force has a voice, a sinister whisper in Lord Druid Douglas' ear, compelling him to feed the Source Stone and driving a wedge between him and his companions. Trath's magic could protect the druid lord, but the prince has fled heartbreak in search of a different life. But will his quest bring redemption or ruin?

Book 6: Age of Druids

Imprisoned by the demons of The Bleak, two lost druids fight to survive while Munro pushes himself to the brink to find them. In his search, he discovers a mysterious gate even the oldest and wisest of the Otherworld fear.

The Halls of Mists are in ruin, and people scheme, grasping at power as a new kingdom emerges and an ancient one reappears. Tragedy pits druid against queen, testing friendship, loyalty, and love once more.

Who will survive and who will be lost forever as desperation drives some to unthinkable ends?

CPSIA information can be obtained at www.ICGtesting.com
Printed in the USA
LVOW06s1705121015

457920LV00001B/62/P